WITHDRAWN

FROM

STOCK

FEUD AT GRECO CANYON

By the same author

Dead Man Smiling
Colorado Runaround
The Major and the Miners
Five Deadly Shadows
Montana Crisis
Rooney's Second Deputy

Feud at Greco Canyon

LEONARD MEARES

ROBERT HALE · LONDON

First published in Great Britain 1994

ISBN 0 7090 5175 1

Robert Hale Limited
Clerkenwell House
Clerkenwell Green
London EC1R 0HT

Photoset in North Wales by
Derek Doyle & Associates, Mold, Clwyd.
Printed and bound in Great Britain by
WBC Ltd, Bridgend, Mid-Glamorgan.

1

The Available Braddocks

It was 10.15 of a crisp spring morning when Hattie Braddock, distaff half of the Braddock Detective Agency, bustled into the Quinn Brothers Tonsorial Parlour.

To find her husband, blonde and beautiful Hattie had only to descend the side stairs from the five-room apartment above the barber shop; the Quinn brothers were the Braddocks' landlords. Right now, handsome Rick Braddock was having his dark hair trimmed by Ernie Quinn who, like his brother and the other customers, greeted Hattie with admiring grins. Well, Ernie and Herb Quinn aimed the admiring grins. The customer in Herb's chair and the three waiting did some overt ogling.

'Too late, boys,' she good-humouredly announced. 'I belong to another.'

'Careful, gents,' warned Ernie. 'This is Rick Braddock in my chair, the lady's lucky husband.'

'Don't get too eager,' advised Herb. 'Rick could put all of you down without working up a sweat.'

'You can admire,' Rick invited. 'Just don't touch.' He traded affectionate smiles with his wife.

'Looking for me, honey? Ernie'll be through with me pretty soon.'

'Couldn't wait to tell you,' she said. She was still being ogled, and small wonder. The city of Denver, Colorado, boasted few women who could match her blonde, blue-eyed beauty and her perfect figure. 'We've received an invitation, delivered by hand if you please, special messenger from the Hotel Carlton.'

'The Carlton, huh?' Ernie Quinn was impressed. 'Best hotel in the whole city.'

'Caters to the carriage trade,' his brother said knowledgeably. 'Anybody stays at the Carlton, they got to be rich. I mean *real* rich.'

'Rick, you'll never guess who sent the invitation,' smiled Hattie.

'Invitation to a high stake poker party?' he asked. 'I'm in the mood for *that*.'

'Something a little more sedate,' she replied. 'Afternoon tea.'

'With?' he asked.

'Mister and Mrs Charles D. Hargrove,' she announced.

Ernie Quinn whistled and rolled his eyes.

'Careful with those scissors,' begged Rick.

'You never heard of 'em?' challenged Ernie. 'Holy Moses, Rick. Charles D. Hargrove Junior – heir to the whole shebang, the Topeka and Western Banking Company, branches all over Kansas, Colorado, Utah, all the way to the west coast, an outfit near as big as the First National!'

'Sounds encouraging,' remarked Rick. 'We just might be attracting a better class of client, Hattie.'

His haircut finished, he paid Ernie and donned his coat. Had Hattie not been the only woman present, the others might have ogled her husband as enthusiastically as she had been ogled. Rick was a well-built six-footer, dark-eyed and as handsome as they come. He had poise, fine manners and, like his wife, a chequered background.

Arm in arm, the Braddocks quit the barber shop and climbed the stairs to their apartment. They were a young couple, but had done more living than folk twice their age; both had come up the hard way.

Before meeting and marrying Hattie and establishing this two-operative detective agency, Rick had been bewilderingly versatile. He had been befriended when an orphaned boy by a well-educated con man who had taught him much. By the tender age of sixteen, he was an experienced ranch-hand and prospector. He had worked with many a travelling repertory group and carnival show, honing a flair for character acting, could play several musical instruments, spoke fluent Spanish and a smattering of French and had even worked a trick-shooting act. As if that wasn't enough versatility for any one man, he was expert at all games of chance; his poker tutor had been a veteran riverboat gambler.

As confidential investigators, Rick and Hattie were living well and earning better than expenses. As husband and wife, they were a perfect match, for her past had been as varied as his. Only issue of the union of a frontier schoolmaster and a music teacher, she had been orphaned in her early teens and, until getting together with Rick, had supported herself every which way. From seamstress, nursemaid and waitress, she had gone on to join tent shows and, like Rick, travelling theatre groups. While Rick was gaining experience, so was Hattie, sometimes performing as magician's assistant, chorus girl, knife-thrower's assistant, but at her best when cast in melodramas, playing any role offered, often the *ingénue*, sometimes child roles and, thanks to her skill at make-up and characterization, even grandmothers. If she were the bragging kind, she could justly claim, as could Rick, that she had 'done it all'.

In the room doing double duty as their parlour and office, she offered the invitation for her husband's appraisal. It was as much a request as an invitation. Certainly it was graciously phrased. Fine quality paper. Graceful handwriting. Judith Hargrove and her husband would be most grateful if Mr and Mrs R.J. Braddock would take afternoon tea with them this day, three o'clock, Suite 28, Hotel Carlton, Barrier Street. If this proved convenient, please inform the courier accordingly.

'You told the messenger we accept,' he guessed.

'We'll be free,' she said. 'And I'm predicting an assignment, a new case for us and a handsome retainer. We aren't acquainted. Why else would they send for us?'

'An assignment for sure,' Rick agreed. 'They'll have seen our ad in all the Denver papers.'

'Wealthy folk – big money,' enthused Hattie. 'We'd better do this in style, best foot forward. You'll wear your dark blue suit.'

'We have ample time to buy you a new gown,' he decided.

'Let nobody call my beloved husband a tightwad,' she chuckled. 'Darling, my wardrobe is *bulging*. I have clothes for every occasion and plenty of them.'

While they were at lunch, Rick waxed confident, his brain working like a cash register.

'It'll be something big,' he opined. 'Big problem, big fee. Whatever it is, we'll handle it. After the payout, how'd you like a vacation? Anywhere you please, honey. Chicago? New York?'

'Let's discuss that later,' Hattie suggested. 'All I'm thinking about right now is the big question. What could the Hargroves want of us? People so wealthy could afford to retain the Pinkertons. They have influence in high places, Rick. The government for instance. I've heard Hargrove senior's on first name terms with senators, congressmen....'

'Something delicate maybe,' said Rick. He grinned and winked. 'A little family matter they're reluctant to confide to their political connections.'

'So they prefer to rely on the discretion of a smaller concern?' she mused. 'You could be right, my dear. A distinct possibility.'

'For a smaller concern, we've won good publicity,' he reminded her. 'We're becoming known since the Shayville deal and the rumpus at Granger City. The newspapers gave us big coverage.'

'I still say it was wise of us to refuse to be photographed,' she declared. 'For our own purposes, the kind of cases we've broken, we're safer where we can't be recognized. We can disguise ourselves – often do – but do we have to do that every time?'

'Depends on the situation,' he agreed.

As was typical of the Braddocks, they travelled to Barrier Street by cab and, when entering the spacious, thick-carpeted lobby of Denver's most luxurious hotel, gave the impression they were well accustomed to such de luxe refinery. Hattie had chosen a maroon gown and matching accessories which included a fashionable *chapeau*. Attended by her sartorially elegant husband, she won admiring glances from all parties present. At the reception desk, Rick offered his card.

'We're expected,' he said calmly. 'Mister and Mrs Hargrove?'

'Ah, Mister and Mrs Braddock,' beamed the clerk. 'Welcome to the Carlton. Boy!'

He snapped his fingers and gave instructions to a uniformed page who led the visitors upstairs to Suite 28 and knocked gently. The door was opened by a man as tall as Rick, expensively garbed, fair haired and almost as handsome. He greeted them courteously, identified himself as their host, shook hands with Rick, kissed Hattie's hand, tipped the page and reminded him, 'Tea.'

'Yes, sir,' said the page. 'Two minutes.'

Charles Hargrove conducted the guests into a tastefully appointed drawing-room and presented them to his wife, who rose gracefully from a *chaise-longue* to smile a warm welcome and extend a hand.

'Judith, my dear, our guests are most punctual,' smiled her husband.

'Thank you both for coming.' Judith Hargrove said this so earnestly that Rick believed she meant it. 'And on such short notice. We're most grateful. Charles and I do realize how busy you must be.'

'Many demands for your services, I'd surmise,' said Charles, as they seated themselves.

'We're kept busy, Mister Hargrove,' nodded Rick. 'But who could refuse such a gracious invitation?'

'You're available at this time – I hope,' Judith said anxiously. She was auburn haired with hazel eyes, an attractive woman with, Rick sensed, a problem. 'It's a matter of some urgency and personal importance to me.'

'The urgency of all matters presented to us is always the deciding factor,' said Rick.

A gentle knock was followed by the arrival of a waiter toting a laden tray which he set on the table and then, after bowing to the Hargroves, quietly withdrew. A silver tea service. Cups and saucers of the finest bone china. Judith poured. The Hargroves and their guests sipped tea and got down to business.

'Judith will explain the situation,' said Charles. 'I, of course, will take care of all the financial details, your expenses etcetera. Ready, my dear?'

'Shouldn't you first explain to Mister and Mrs Braddock why we have such confidence in them?' she suggested.

'Certainly,' he agreed. 'Mister Braddock, you weren't chosen at random. We had ample prior knowledge of your ability as a detective. And, I should add, a man of action capable of taking the initiative in time of crisis. You see, we visited Granger City on the occasion of Miss Ella Cardew's appearance there, her three-night engagement at the Rialto Theatre. Judith has long been an admirer of Miss Cardew's. I, too. She sings beautifully.'

'Her voice is her fortune,' remarked Rick. 'Of course her looks are her other big asset.'

'We had reservations for her third show, the last night,' said Charles. 'It wasn't till next morning, when we were about to leave for our hometown,

Topeka, that we learned of the attempted kidnapping.'

'We were shocked,' frowned Judith. 'But also impressed, Mister Braddock. It was you who got the better of those – those evil men.'

'Newspapers called them the Five Deadly Shadows,' murmured Hattie.

'Well....' Rick shrugged nonchalantly. 'Justice usually triumphs.'

'You're too modest,' chided Charles. 'Single-handedly, you ran those kidnappers to ground and ...'

'I had help,' said Rick.

'Very well, be as modest as you wish,' said Charles. 'But all we learned of that terrible business convinced my wife that you're the man best suited to put an end to the situation that so distresses her.' He set his cup aside. 'Go ahead, my dear. we need have no secrets from these professionals.'

'Discretion guaranteed,' Rick assured him. 'Discretion, and our best efforts.'

'It concerns my father, to whom I'm devoted,' Judith began. 'His name is Edward Whitton and he is sheriff of Greco County, a cattle community to the south-east.'

'Approximately a hundred miles from here,' interjected her husband.

'A veteran law officer, more than twenty years of peacekeeping, years that have taken their toll,' she continued. 'He should retire, but he's so stubborn. When he sets his mind to something – well – my education, my future for instance. After my mother's death, he was determined to provide the best of everything for me. To pay my tuition fees at the Dupont College in Kansas City, he scrimped and saved, borrowed from a Greco bank, even slept in a cell of the county jail to avoid paying room rent at a hotel or boarding-house. Can you wonder I'm so devoted to him? I owe him so much.' She reached for her husband's hand. 'Including the happiest marriage any woman could hope for.'

'If Judith hadn't been a college student in Kansas City, we'd never have met,' Charles explained.

'He could turn his back on it all, come live with us, but he's so ...' began Judith.'

'Stubborn, you said,' nodded Hattie.

'And this is the worst time for a man his age,' fretted Judith. 'So much trouble, more than he can cope with, yet he refuses to give up, insists he won't retire till peace has been restored.'

'From that, I assume Greco's in some kind of turmoil,' said Rick. 'Pardon my interrupting you, Mrs Hargrove, but can you tell me anything about your father's deputies?'

'There are two,' she said. 'I don't remember their names, but Dad assures me they're loyal to him and, naturally, they share his frustration. You see, the threat to the peace is a feud.'

As she talked on, Rick and Hattie easily conjured up a mind picture of the cattletown and its environs. In the vast and verdant Greco Canyon, west of the county seat, the two biggest landholders were a rancher, Buck Brister, and a farmer, Mace Kenrick. Circle B range was separated from Kenrick's fields of wheat and corn by Greco Creek, and the two men, both widowers with grown sons, had been at loggerheads for some time. Shots had been exchanged. Kenrick's sons and hired hands were every inch as belligerent and just as ready with their guns as Brister's sons and his bunkhouse gang. With citizens of the township divided by loyalty to the feuding factions, Sheriff Whitton's problems were multiplying daily.

'And he simply cannot cope, Mister Braddock,' declared Judith. 'The worry, the constant strain, is too much for him. At his age, he could suffer a seizure.' She dabbed at her eyes as her husband placed a comforting hand on her shoulder. 'He's been such a generous and caring father – I can't bear the thought of his dying of a heart attack. He's a good man. When his times comes – he has earned a peaceful death in a comfortable bed – at peace with his Maker – his mind at rest....'

'Compose yourself – take your time,' soothed Charles. To the Braddocks he remarked, 'I'm as concerned as Judith. Her father made the journey to Topeka for our wedding, and I can assure you he's as fine, as decent a man as Judith has told you. My parents hold him in high regard and, speaking for myself, I'm proud to be his son-in-law.'

'Rough-spoken, a gruff-voiced old man,' sighed Judith. 'But a gentleman at heart and always fair.'

'He sounds like the old-time lawmen I've always respected,' Rick said tactfully. 'Dedicated. Incorruptible.'

'That's Dad, that's Red Ed Whitton,' she nodded. 'I inherited my mother's nature, all her attitudes. In appearance, I strongly resemble her, Dad always says. Where looks are concerned – Mother was dark-haired so, as you can see....'

'Your father's auburn hair,' smiled Hattie.

'Greying fast, I fear,' Judith lamented.

'Another of the sad traditions of the frontier,' reflected Rick. 'Cattlemen in bitter rivalry against farmers. If not farmers, sheepmen.'

'If you can succeed where Judith's father has failed, devise some means of bringing the feud to an end....' Having said that, Charles paused a moment. 'It must seem an impossible task. We could hardly blame you if....'

'Not at all, Mister Hargrove,' said Rick. 'The seemingly impossible can sometimes be achieved.'

'It wouldn't be the first feud we've investigated,' Hattie reminded him. 'There's always a way, Rick. We just have to find that way.'

'We?' asked Charles.

'My wife is also my associate, my partner,' offered Rick. 'I acknowledge that with pride, believe me. In her own right, Hattie is a wily investigator.'

Judith was deeply impressed.

'What a sensible arrangement,' she said approvingly, 'in an age when decision-making is usually considered the husband's prerogative.'

'My dear Mrs Hargrove,' grinned Rick, 'your husband and I married intelligent ladies.'

'We have that in common, sir,' agreed Charles. 'And how I wish *I* could help solve my father-in-law's problems. but every man to his calling, isn't that so? Banking is my business. Yours is the detection and solving of criminal and other anti-social predicaments.'

'Your opinion?' Rick asked Hattie.

'You've already decided,' she said. 'So have I. It'll be a challenge to our ingenuity, Rick, but one of us – probably you – will think of a new approach. I suppose the first detail we'll be seeking is the cause.'

'That's where we'll begin,' decided Rick. 'What started all the ill-feeling? Yes, find the cause, then do something about it.'

'This is wonderful,' exclaimed Judith. 'I anticipated you'd have to be persuaded.' Fervently, she gave thanks. 'If you can help in any way, I'll be indebted to you the rest of my life.'

'It means a great deal to Judith, and to me.' Her husband was just as sincere. 'I had thought of retaining the Pinkerton Agency but, with both of us remembering the Granger City incident, we felt that an appeal to you would be the wiser course. Call it instinct, Mister Braddock, but I believe this is your kind of case. As your charming wife put it, a challenge. And now to more practical considerations....'

It *was* inevitable the Braddocks would take the case. Rick wasn't given to nominate a fee. Charles Braddock insisted money was no problem, produced an impressive sum in cash and called it a retainer. He then asked if $65 per day plus expenses would be acceptable to them.

'Well, I'm sure ...' began Hattie.

'Meaning sixty-five for each of you, a hundred and thirty per day,' Charles hastened to assure her. 'And, when you've settled the feud, there'll be a bonus, naturally.'

Poker-faced, Rick replied, 'That would be quite satisfactory. Hattie will now write you a receipt and, if we may have your home address, you'll receive progress reports after we reach Greco and begin our investigations.'

'Dad would be indignant if he ever learned I'd appealed for outside help,' warned Judith.

'He'll never know,' Rick told her. 'We certainly won't announce our true profession upon our arrival. It'll be an undercover operation.'

'We'll use aliases,' explained Hattie. 'We'll pose as – any ideas, Rick?'

'A bartender seeking a job, an out-of-work nursemaid, whatever we decide before starting for Greco,' shrugged Rick. 'Maybe in disguise, maybe not. We'll probably agree to keep our marital status a secret. I may pass myself off as Hattie's father, for instance.' As the Hargroves' eyebrows shot up, he added, 'That would present no difficulties. We've had considerable theatrical experience.'

'Imagination – resourcefulness!' Charles enthused to his wife. 'They instil confidence, Judith!'

'I feel better about everything now,' she smiled. 'Thank you both, from the bottom of my heart.'

When the Braddocks were rising to take their leave, Charles asked, 'How soon can you begin? We're booked on the evening eastbound from the railroad depot. And you?'

'We'll check maps and timetables, be on our way to Greco as soon as possible and by the fastest route,' Rick promised.

Outside the hotel, while Rick was helping her into a cab, Hattie insisted, 'The bank first. We have to make a deposit.' Rick climbed in beside her and gave directions to the driver. 'That's quite a retainer he gave you. We'll need cash for expenses, but not *that* much.'

'The bank first,' he agreed. 'Then the railroad depot and, if needs be, the Wells Fargo office.'

By the time they had returned to their apartment, they had booked passage. Departing noon tomorrow, a southbound train would take them to Mendoza Junction, where they would board a stagecoach for the last leg of their journey to Greco.

Hattie shook her head to her husband's offer of supper at Charpiot's.

'We're dining home tonight,' she said firmly. 'Plans, Rick. Strategy. Better we stick to our routine. We never yet began an assignment without preparation. It's another undercover operation, don't forget.'

Rick guessed, when they were settling down to their evening meal, 'You'd sooner we stayed closer this time.'

'And not so heavily disguised,' said Hattie. 'We're both wary about showing up in Greco as husband and wife, but need we pretend to be strangers?'

'Two old friends?'

'Something like that.'

'Sounds fine to me. We could check on work prospects in saloons. As we've always said, a saloon's just the place for gathering information. And we need a lot of information, sweetheart, far more than the Hargroves could offer.'

'You want to play piano in some saloon again, the way you did in Shayville?'

'There are other possibilities. Might be an opening for a tableman. I can deal any game of chance you could name, so why not?'

'It'd be kind of nice if we could both work the same saloon. I'd like for us to be in closer contact this time.'

'So we arrive together and, while finding myself a spot, I look for something for you. Like to be an entertainer again?'

'A good front for us,' approved Hattie. 'You a faro dealer maybe, me the singin' gal. What'll you call yourself?'

When an alias was needed, Rick could devise one

on the spot.

'I'll be Sam Gavin, an old pro,' he decided. 'Won't need make-up at all. How about you?'

'I'm your friend Connie Ross,' Hattie said promptly. 'We've worked many a saloon together. But I think I should make just one change.'

'Want to be a redhead like Judy Hargrove?'

'Better a black wig I think.'

'You'll have 'em drooling, honey. We'd *better* work the same saloon – so I'll be on hand to protect you from cowhands enslaved by your beauty.'

'Do you ever tire of flattering me?'

'It hasn't happened yet.'

'I hope it never does.'

'It won't.'

Over dessert, they held hands and traded affectionate smiles.

'The secret of our success,' she said softly. 'Rick loves Hattie as much as Hattie loves Rick.'

'For married folk, you have to admit that's a mighty handy arrangement,' he grinned.

As always, they packed with care, changes of clothing, not just underwear and such, but apparel potentially useful should either of them need a disguise. Their make-up boxes and several wigs were included; they would never embark on an assignment without those tools of trade.

By bedtime, their trunks had been delivered to the railroad depot. Rick, as was his wont, would take his two handguns along, the Colt .45 that would gird his loins, the Smith & Wesson .38 with its special harness and armpit holster. He had found, on more than one hectic occasion, that a hideaway pistol was a handy, sometimes life-saving back-up. When they boarded the southbound at noon of the morrow, they would carry only their valises.

The Braddocks were as ready as they would ever be.

11 a.m. of the next day, while Rick and Hattie were downing a cup of coffee before leaving their Denver headquarters. Judith Hargrove's father was accosted by a local merchant on the main street of Greco, the troubled town far to the south-east.

Skinny Seth Arundell owned one of Greco's biggest general stores. He was sharp-nosed and hatchet-jawed and his mood was mean. In his indignation, he dared shake a finger at the veteran lawman known as Red Ed.

'I'm still mad about it all,' he scowled. 'It's three days since two Kenrick ploughboys and a couple of Circle B hands got into a fight in my place and caused damage, a lot of damage!'

Ed Whitton hooked gnarled thumbs in his gunbelt and matched Arundell's stare unflinchingly. Had his gentle daughter been able to see him at this moment, she might have been less concerned for the state of his health. He was a bulky man who, in the rough garb of his choice, could have been mistaken for a hard-nosed veteran ranch foreman. He stood a shade under six feet and none of his bulk was fat. His was a blunt-featured visage. There were crows' feet at the outer corners of the eyes as hazel as his daughter's and, true, there were grey flecks in the bushy brows and moustache and as much of his thatch as was visible under his battered Stetson. He was no youngster; there could be no denying that. But he was wearing well, his nerves weren't frayed and he was as formidable a law officer as when, long years before, he had first worn a badge.

Gruffly, and with more than a hint of truculence, he reminded Arundell. 'After Deputy Schumack broke up that ruckus and sent them scrappers on their way, I personally demanded Kenrick and Brister should make good on all the damage, and I know for a fact they did.'

'That's small comfort for my customers scared near out of their wits by all that brawling,' retorted Arundell. 'It could happen again any time. You'd better remember, Ed Whitton, I'm a councilman. If you and your deputies can't keep those rowdies in line, don't count on being re-elected next year.'

'Some of the other council men, includin' Mayor Ventry himself, might have somethin' to say about that,' growled Whitton.

'Damn it, things're getting worse all the time,' complained the storekeeper. 'If you don't soon put a stop to the feud in the canyon, this whole county'll be involved in a range war.'

'Doin' everything I can think of,' declared Whitton. 'I fret about it more'n anybody else. You think that feud's my idea of a good time?'

'The citizens're demanding action,' insisted Arundell. 'And, if you're not equal to the task ...'

'Before you finish what you were gonna say, I'll remind you of some other trouble you had,' Whitton said grimly. 'A year and a half ago as I recall. Couple driftin' hard-cases stopped by your store, poked a gun in your kisser and made off with every dollar in your cashbox.'

'Look, I'm not forgetting ...'

'Schumack was laid up with some kind of fever and Dewkes was out of town, deliverin' a prisoner to the Dyer County law, so who took off after them sonsabitches, who headed 'em off this side of the county line, who shot it out with 'em and fetched 'em back here, got his ass bullet-burned, and handed back the cash they robbed you of?'

'I'm not saying you aren't a hard-working sheriff,' winced Arundell.

'I'm mighty obliged.' Whitton resorted to heavy sarcasm. 'That takes a big load off my mind.'

With that, he turned his back on Arundell and moved along Main Street. The county seat's longest thoroughfare ran from east to west. Whitton trudged west, his destination the Oriental Saloon. He wasn't seeking liquid solace, not at this time of day, but a cup of barkeep Billy Conlan's good coffee would be welcome right now.

There was nothing oriental about the decor of Clint Jarrow's place of business, just the pagoda-like ornament atop the sign facing the street. Moving into the big bar-room, the sheriff made his way through the late morning customers to hook a heel on the brass rail, prop an elbow on the edge of the bar and trade nods with the chubby dispenser of cheer.

Conlan filled a cup to the brim.

'On the house, Ed. You're full of worries, I can tell. Well, you ain't the only one.' He gestured to his dapper, moon-faced boss, now joining them. 'Clint's grievin' too.'

''Mornin', Clint,' sighed Whitton. 'Tell me your troubles. You might's well. Every other citizen does.'

2

Passengers En Route

Long a Greco identity, the sheriff was on first-name terms with a great many locals, including saloonkeepers and their staffs and, for that matter, every hotel clerk, every hostler of every livery stable in town. Of the saloonkeepers, pudgy Clint Jarrow was one of his favourites; he knew Jarrow ran an honest house.

'I'm losing my best dealer today, Ed,' Jarrow said dolefully. 'Dick Royce. Name any game, he could deal it. A good friend too. But he's quit and he'll be leaving on the noon stage headed east.'

'Hell, Clint, you can't afford to let him go, not an old hand like Royce,' protested Whitton.

'Dick's decision,' grouched Jarrow. 'I know he's doing it for my sake. You know what I mean. For the good of the Oriental's reputation. Don't have to remind you I never had a crooked dealer working for me.'

'That's a fact,' remarked the barkeep. 'And Dick always dealt square.'

'So what's this all about?' demanded Whitton.

He grimaced in disgust while listening to

Jarrow's account of the incident that had shaken an honest employee and convinced him he should move on. Last night, one of Buck Brister's sons, twenty-two-year-old Dobie, had imbibed more than he could handle and caused a disturbance at the dice table by accusing the supervisor, Dick Royce, of trickery.

'Always a sore loser, that Dobie,' commented Billy. 'The kinda hothead that ought never be allowed to gamble.'

'He claimed Dick had switched to loaded dice – can you beat that?' muttered Jarrow. 'Dick tried to reason with him, invited young Brister to check all the dice, even invited him to search him. But that damn fool roughed him up.'

'You should've called in Nate or Chris,' scowled Whitton.

'The deputy on duty can't be in a dozen places at one time,' shrugged Jarrow. 'Well, as you know, Dick's a small man and no fighter and all the Brister boys, all three of 'em, pack a lot of muscle.'

'Mace Kenrick's sons too,' interjected the barkeep.

'Dick wasn't seriously injured,' continued Jarrow. 'Dobie backhanded him and belly-punched him. The thing is, the whole incident shook him. And he was always loyal to me, Ed. He figured Dobie'd put it around that he was a sharper and such talk'd be bad for the Oriental's reputation. So he's doing it voluntarily – just quitting.'

'The hell with it,' breathed Whitton.

'Good housemen're hard to find,' said Jarrow. 'Dick'll be hard to replace.'

'It won't help you much but, for what it's worth, I'll warn Dobie Brister to be careful how much booze he puts away and to tight-rein that damn temper of his,' promised Whitton. 'Next time I lay eyes on him, that's what I'll be doin'. And, if he's with his father and the other two Brister boys, it'll still be said.'

'Losing Dick's my problem right now,' said Jarrow. 'Your problem's bigger, Ed.'

'I know it,' Whitton sourly assured him. 'And I wish I knew the answer to the big question – how to convince Brister and Kenrick they can live in peace, work their land and be good neighbours – 'stead of tradin' lead from both sides of the creek? Both of 'em, Buck Brister and Mace Kenrick, mule-stubborn. And they got no real reason for feudin'. Plenty graze for Circle B cattle east of the creek, and Kenrick owns all the land he can farm.'

'Old Mace ain't no two-bit sodbuster,' reflected Billy. 'Got near as many farmhands workin' for him as Buck's got cowhands. And, like Buck's men, them ploughboys pack guns and know how to use 'em. Big place, the Kenrick farm.'

The sheriff's mood was still grim when, at lunchtime, he shared a table at Tulloch's Café with a local doctor, another Greco Canyon rancher and that rancher's foreman.

Nobody had ever convinced scrawny, sharp-featured Ansell Frickett, MD, that frontier medicos should be good humoured, tolerant and philosophical, never grumpy. Frickett seemed surly twenty-four hours of every day of the year. He could, if he made the effort, show compassion for some of his patients, a frightened child for instance, maybe a woman experiencing her first pregnancy. But he was derisive of nine-tenths of the county population.

'The trouble will never end,' he predicted while Whitton munched on fried chicken. 'Try talking horse sense to any of the belligerents and you'll only be wasting your breath, Ed Whitton. I can't comment on the intelligence of Buck Brister or Mace Kenrick – don't know them well enough – but I regard all muscle-bound farmhands and trigger-happy cowboys as jack-asses, simpletons, idiots always spoiling for a fight.'

There were smaller ranches in the canyon. Luther Prowse owned one of them. Short-bearded and heavyset, he bossed Bar 9. The just as hefty man keeping him company at this time was his foreman, Rex Abelson. Prowse voiced sympathy for Whitton's predicament, declaring he didn't envy him the chore of trying to keep the peace in a period when a range war seemed inevitable.

'But I'm worried too,' he told Whitton. 'And I guess I'm speakin' for the other ranchers. What we fear is we'll all be under attack if Mace Kenrick hires gunhawks to patrol his acres.'

'He could afford to,' opined Abelson. 'He's near as rich as Buck Brister, raises fine crops and, after harvest-time, sells it for top dollar.'

'Just as Brister grows richer after every round-up, every trail-drive to Cahill City and the railhead,' muttered Whitton.

'I've appealed to 'em both, you know,' offered Prowse.

'No,' said Whitton, jabbing with his fork. 'I didn't know that. Appealed to 'em, huh? I've tried talkin' sense to 'em oftener'n I can keep count. And it's like talkin' to deaf men. They just won't *listen*.'

'Well, my spread's closest to Circle B,' Prowse pointed out. 'And, if it comes to a shootin' war, Bar could get caught in the crossfire.' He shrugged helplessly. 'Greco Canyon land's plenty fertile, what with the creek snakin' all through it. Plenty water for all of us. It could be a peaceful place for cattlemen *and* Kenrick.'

'Anybody been snipin' at your hired hands?' asked Whitton.

'Not yet, but it *could* happen,' fretted Prowse.

'Our nighthawks ride nervous,' said Abelson. 'Helluva situation, Sheriff.'

'As if anybody needs to remind me,' scowled Whitton.

After their train journey south to Mendoza Junction, the Braddocks' baggage was transferred to the stagecoach that would take them to Greco. They had to wait only one hour before boarding and, when the stage rolled out of Mendoza Junction, there were three other passengers, an elderly couple bound for Cahill City and a plain-faced spinster who informed them she too was headed for Greco.

The older folk weren't in the mood for conversation with strangers, seemed more intent on dozing. But Miss Minerva Platt was nervous and needing friendly ears. Now a brunette with make-up to back the illusion, and somewhat gaudily gowned, Hattie was well in character in her role of saloon singer. Miss Minerva didn't seem leery of her, probably because Hattie's smile was reassuring. And the spinster, who described herself as a schoolteacher after introductions were exchanged, could not fault the manners of the sartorially elegant Mr Sam Gavin, the sporting gentleman. Sharing the forward seat with Rick and

Hattie, she nervously confided that she was already regretting having accepted the position of new teacher at the Greco County School.

She had been a teacher all her adult life and wished she were still teaching at Mendoza Junction, which had been her hometown several years.

'But you couldn't stay on?' asked Hattie.

'I was obliged to resign,' frowned Minerva. 'There was an advertisement in a Greco paper, which circulates over quite a wide area, inviting applications for the position there. I applied and Mayor Josiah Ventry, who seems a really nice gentleman, replied to inform me the job was mine and accommodation had been arranged for me at a respectable boarding-house.'

'And now, Miss Platt, you have misgivings?' prodded Rick.

'After I telegraphed Mayor Ventry to advise him of my date of arrival, another issue of the *Greco Times* reached Mendoza Junction,' said Minerva. 'And what I read disturbed me. You and Miss Ross hope to find work there, you said. Did you know the Greco community is suffering great upheaval? There has been violence, Mister Gavin. A rancher and a farmer, both wealthy men, have practically declared war on each other. It's a feud, and the antagonists command large forces of armed men. A terrible state of affairs, so why *wouldn't* I have misgivings? I can't even be sure people are safe on the streets.'

'Oh, the feud,' Hattie said offhandedly.

'We've heard talk of it, Miss Platt, but I doubt you need worry,' shrugged Rick. 'We may rely on the county law officers to maintain control of the situation.'

'I hope so,' sighed Minerva. 'I most certainly hope so.'

'You afraid Greco's last schoolma'am was scared out of town?' challenged Hattie.

'Well, no,' said Minerva. 'In his letter, Mayor Ventry explained she resigned her position after marrying a travelling salesman resident in Denver.' Apprehensively, she admitted to the amiable entertainer and the courtly gambler, 'It's the children I'm most worried about. My pupils may be caught up in the rivalry, supporting the rancher or the farmer and – behaving aggressively. I'm a conscientious teacher and can control smaller children but, as you can see, I'm a small person. How could I hope to separate brawling boys – big boys?'

'Too bad you had to quit Mendoza Junction,' remarked Hattie.

'I had to,' said Minerva. 'There was no other way.' A moment of hesitation. Bemused, Rick and Hattie waited. 'You see, I was being courted.'

Rick took his cue and played the gallant. At that, his compliment was sincere. Though plain of face, Minerva Platt was not without appeal. The small figure was neat, her travelling gown fashionable enough and in good taste.

'I can well understand,' he declared, 'any discerning gentleman paying court to a lady of your quality.'

'He was most persistent,' complained Minerva. 'And I'm afraid "gentleman" is not the word for him. To my great distress, I discovered he was already married. His children were enrolled at the school and – apparently his wife knew nothing of his – his....'

'Roving eye,' supplied Hattie.

'I was horrified,' murmured Minerva. 'I simply could not continue to live in the same town with such a person.'

'The blackguard,' said Rick.

'Cheating husbands,' sneered Hattie. 'The worst kind. Bottom of the barrel.'

'Be of good heart, dear lady,' soothed Rick. 'My good friend Connie and I are incurable optimists. I strongly recommend optimism. In Greco County, the law will prevail, mark my words.'

'We've heard talk of the county sheriff,' Hattie told the schoolteacher. 'Good man. It might take him a little time to settle that feud, but he'll figure a way.'

'I'm not always so open with strangers,' said Minerva. 'When not engaged in my work, I tend to be reticent. You sing in saloons? I never met anybody like you before and, in fact, Mister Gavin is the first – uh – sporting gentleman with whom I've ever had a conversation. I must say you are both very reassuring and patient, and I do appreciate that.'

'We're a mixed bunch,' shrugged Hattie.

'It takes all kinds,' Rick said casually. 'For our part, we appreciate your taking us into your confidence.'

'Better you talked of it anyway,' smiled Hattie. 'Better than keeping all your fears bottled up.'

'By the time we reach Greco ...' began Minerva.

'Noon, day after tomorrow,' said Rick.

'... I may feel a little less apprehensive.' Minerva managed a brief smile. 'Thanks to your encouragement.'

The stage rolled into Greco on schedule; it was

high noon when Rick helped Hattie and the schoolteacher alight and, while the guard and a depot-hand unloaded their baggage, the small woman was greeted by the urbane Mayor Ventry and a member of the school board. Rick, involved in taking delivery of two valises, and Hattie arranging for their trunks to be loaded on to a pushcart for transfer to a hotel, were unaware one of Whitton's deputies was at the depot at this time.

Showing more than casual interest in the schoolteacher was Chris Dewkes. Aged twenty-eight, he was the younger of the sheriff's aides and had never been called handsome, but the face under the mid-brown hair was sensitive-featured. In build, he was hefty, a six-footer, broad of shoulders and chest who, like his boss and the other deputy, was rarely seen in town clothes. So there he was. Not ogling the small woman. Not his style. Just studying her solemnly.

At the Hubbard Hotel, the Braddocks registered as S. Gavin and C. Ross and checked into upstairs rooms, rear singles side by side with windows opening on to the gallery. Soon thereafter, they were at lunch in the hotel's dining-room and discussing their next move. It was agreed that, when they were through eating, Hattie would do some unpacking while Rick canvassed the local saloons.

'You'd better get lucky, lover,' she quietly warned. 'We've arrived looking like Lulu the black-haired singin' gal and a dude sportin' gent, so it has to be a saloon.'

'It's a big town with saloons all over the place,' Rick pointed out. 'Don't worry, I'll find us a spot.'

'Whatever you can manage for us,' she urged. 'It

doesn't have to be the fanciest joy-house in town, just so long as there're gambling layouts and a piano. Check a mirror and you'll see we look like what we're supposed to be. We've arrived, we've been seen, so it's too late for you to pretend you're a ranch-hand or for me to look for work slinging hash or nursemaiding kids.'

'I'll be keeping that in mind,' he assured her. 'Just leave it to me, honey. We're a cinch.'

'Now you're talking,' she approved. 'Give it that old Braddock know-how. Oops. Should've said the Gavin touch.'

When Rick emerged from the hotel some time later, he walked only a half-block of Main Street before coming upon a scene bound to spur him to action. He was drawing near to the sheriff's office fronting the county jail. A pretty girl in calico was about to climb the steps to the office porch when a wagon stalled out front. Two brawny young men promptly dropped from the rig and seized her and, as she began to struggle, Rick dashed to her rescue. From his viewpoint, this was attempted abduction and, being over-supplied with gallantry, what the hell else was he going to do?

They were dragging her toward the wagon when he descended on them. He grasped a wrist and twisted it, breaking the hold of the man who had gripped the girl's arm. The other one glowered at him and swung a punch.

'Move clear, little lady,' he urged as he parried the blow and retaliated.

The puncher backstepped and flopped on his backside, his nose bloody. Whitton and his senior deputy, the lean, droopy-moustached Nate Schumack, moved out on to the porch as the other hard-case swung two hard ones at the newcomer. Had either of them connected, Rick would have been in trouble, but this was his kind of action. He dodged, ducked and jabbed and, gasping, his adversary sprawled on the sidewalk. The elderly man in charge of the team scowled ferociously and made to descend from the seat.

'No fancy pants is gonna get away with...!'

'Stay right where you are,' Rick sharply commanded. 'There are quite a few years between us. I don't want to use force on a man your age, but you'd better believe I won't stand by and see these roughnecks abduct a defenceless girl.'

'Hey, hero.' Whitton addressed him gruffly from atop the steps. 'You're talkin' to the girl's father and the two you clobbered are her brothers – not that I'm blamin' you for gettin' the wrong idea.'

'I love Phil,' cried the girl. 'I don't care who knows it and – and I only want to visit him. If I'd guessed Pa or Jethro or Orin'd read my mind and follow me to town, I wouldn't have come.'

'Ain't blamin' you for this either, young Martha,' said Whitton. 'But I ain't got the authority to come between father and daughter.' He stared hard at the man on the driver's seat. 'Mace Kenrick, what harm would it do, lettin' her see him, if that's how she feels about young Brister?'

'I call that a mighty foolish question, Whitton.' The farmer spoke bitterly as his sons began rising groggily and while Rick's mind buzzed with questions. 'Joe Siddons worked for me five years and he was a good man. Last night, while he was ridin' guard – you know all this, so I oughtn't have to tell it again – young Brister backshot him. My boy Jethro ...' He indicated the loser with the bloody nose, '... heard the shot, forded the creek, chased that no-good killer and caught him, then delivered him to you fair and square. It's murder, by damn, and Phil Brister'll pay for it and I'll not let my only daughter anywhere near a killer, specially a backshootin' ...'

'Phil *couldn't* be guilty!' Martha Kenrick heatedly protested. 'He's good and decent and...!'

'Into the wagon!' ordered her father. 'Orin, if you're through pokin' that kerchief in your mouth and gettin' it all bloody, find her horse and tie it back of the rig. We're goin' home.'

The girl was weeping now. Gently, Whitton assured her, 'The young feller's plenty worried, Martha, but behavin' himself and gettin' fed regular. I'll tell him you wanted to see him.'

Regaining their feet, the brothers growled threats at Rick. There'd be a next time, if he was fool enough to stay in Greco. They weren't about to forget him. Any dude daring to tangle with them was begging for trouble. To these threats, Rick coldly countered, 'If you're waiting for me to tremble in fear, don't hold your breath.'

Orin Kenrick fetched his sister's pony and tied it behind the wagon. She was lifted by her other brother and dumped on the seat beside her father, who growled at the team and turned them. Orin scrambled over the tailgate as their rig completed its turn. Then the Kenricks were westbound and Rick was trading appraisals with the sheriff and reflecting that, when Judith Hargrove was agitated, she was apt to exaggerate. This was obvious to him as he studied the burly boss-lawman. Red Ed Whitton close to despair, weakened by his fears of open warfare between the

Kenricks and Bristers, in danger of suffering a seizure? Not likely. Not this hard-eyed, durable man, looking rough enough, tough enough, to beat hell out of double his weight in troublemakers.

He identified himself by his alias and acknowledged his error.

'You should've thought twice, Gavin,' drawled Deputy Schumack, touching a match to a well-chewed stogie. 'If any galoots were gonna kidnap a girl, would they do it right outside the sheriff's office?'

'Quite right,' nodded Rick. 'I should've thought twice. I acted impulsively, just reacted, I guess.'

'Sportin' man on the drift,' Whitton grumpily surmised. 'Lookin' for a high stake poker party.'

'Looking for work, regular work,' corrected Rick. 'I can deal any game you could name and have never been accused of cheating, except by a few sore losers.'

'And you gunned 'em down,' growled Whitton, his gaze fixing on Rick's tied-down .45.

'No, I'm not trigger-happy,' Rick assured him. 'Only their teeth were damaged.'

'Tough *hombre*,' grunted Schumack.

'I could use a job,' said Rick. 'My preference is a saloon where gambling operations are run honestly, some square deal establishment. And who better than the sheriff would know of such a place?'

Whitton ran a jaundiced eye over him and jerked a thumb.

'Might be a spot for you at the Oriental. This side of the street, two blocks east.'

Strolling Main Street again, Rick studied this sprawling cattletown and the citizens out and about and sensed the prevailing atmosphere. Some folk appeared relaxed; nevertheless there was tension here, an air of expectancy. So one of the big shot cattleman's sons had been charged with the murder of one of Mace Kenrick's hired hands. A new development, a new complication. The situation was becoming even more incendiary.

And the Romeo and Juliet factor, he reflected. The daughter of one rival in love with the son of the other. Just what we needed, I don't think. Complications!

But first things first. He and Hattie needed to establish themselves here, so his pitch to the owner of the Oriental had better be persuasive.

He wasn't to know that his pitch was bound to succeed, Clint Jarrow having lost a houseman not yet replaced. In the bar-room doing a fair trade in the pre-lunch hour, Jarrow gave him a good hearing, asked a question or two and expressed his satisfaction.

'Any pro putting the arm on me would have to deal square, Gavin,' he declared. 'My place has a reputation and every operator I put on my payroll's duty bound to uphold that reputation. Rule of the house.'

'Let me put it this way,' offered Rick. 'I admire sharpers as much as I'd admire a backshooter or a woman-beater.'

'I guess you'll do,' decided Jarrow. 'You can start tonight?'

'Certainly. What time?'

'Make it a quarter before seven. Now I'll show you the layouts and introduce you to the rest of the outfit.'

Rick, after ingratiating himself with the table-hands, the bartenders and Jarrow's two hired girls, nudged the saloonkeeper and gestured to another employee. The age of the derby-hatted character performing at the upright piano was anybody's guess. Except for the moustache, grey like his hair, he was clean-shaven. Baggy under his eyes, but no age-lines criss-crossing the face. Again, Jarrow introduced Sam Gavin, this time to the affable piano player, Waldo Gooch.

'You play well, Waldo,' Rick complimented him. Then to Jarrow, 'Either of your hired girls sing to the trade?'

'Madge and Allie coax the customers to the gambling layouts, dance with them or just listen to their woes – mostly about wives who don't understand them,' said Jarrow. 'But, when it comes to singing....'

'No idea of time or tone,' mumbled Waldo. 'Not exactly easy on the ears, you know?'

'Got a suggestion for you, Clint,' said Rick. 'OK if I call you Clint? I'm Sam to everybody. Friend of mine came to Greco with me. Name of Connie Ross. We know each other from way back. Singing's her business, Clint, and she's good. A looker too. Natural-born entertainer, and entertainment draws trade. With her on your payroll, I guarantee you'd give the saloons of this town some stiff competition.'

'What's called an added attraction, Clint,' offered Waldo. 'Sam's got a point. Good-looking girl who can carry a tune gets popular fast. I've seen it happen.'

'Well ...' frowned Jarrow.

'Won't cost you a dime to audition her,' urged Rick.

'Audition,' repeated Waldo. 'Haven't heard that word in quite a time. Show-business talk, Clint.'

'We're staying at the same hotel, Hubbard's,' said Rick. 'I could have her here in five minutes, ten at most.'

'I'll listen to her and look her over,' shrugged Jarrow. 'If the customers like her, maybe I'll make her an offer.'

'I'll get right back to you,' said Rick, and hurried out.

A few minutes later, his wife was admitting him to her room and listening to his news.

'Sounds promising,' was her reaction. 'Should I change?'

'You look great just as you are. Do just one song for Clint Jarrow's clientele and we'll both be working at the Oriental.'

'Fine. Showtime again. Let's do it.'

Hattie donned a jaunty hat, took his arm and was escorted to the Oriental, there to be ogled by both staff and customers. Jarrow greeted her cordially, nodded to the piano player and told her, 'That's Waldo. Just name the song, he's bound to know it.'

'Anything, Waldo,' said Hattie, flashing a smile. 'You name it. And the key doesn't matter. High or low, I'll keep up with you.'

'How about "Step Right Up To The Bar, Boys"?' Waldo suggested.

'Give me an intro and away we go,' she invited.

Waldo vamped an introduction, Hattie went into her act and, for the next three and a half minutes, the staff and customers of the Oriental lost interest in conversation, whatever game was being patronized and whatever liquor they'd been drinking. All eyes were on the vividly beautiful, black-haired woman lustily singing the lyrics, strutting from table to table, flashing that winning smile, sometimes patting a face, sometimes coaxing a hypnotized local out of his chair to dance a few steps with her. Waldo was grinning approvingly and providing rhythmic accompaniment, Jarrow nodding in time with the beat and the hired girls, like everybody else, lost in admiration.

For her big finish, Hattie leapt lithely to the bar, perched herself on its outer edge, crossed her legs, spread her arms and held the last note till Waldo's last chord stopped echoing. The Oriental then erupted into deafening applause, locals clapping, whooping, cheering, whistling, pounding tabletops. Rick helped his wife back on to her feet and aimed a bland grin at Jarrow.

Felix Lippert, Greco's undertaker, had never been called demonstrative, nor even excitable. Now, however, that scrawny character in sober black rose and bellowed to the saloonkeeper,

'I give you fair warning, Clinton Jarrow! If one of your competitors hires that Lorelei, you won't see me in here again! I'll be doing my drinking in *his* saloon!'

'Plain enough the whole crowd feels that way about you,' Jarrow remarked to Hattie. He made her an offer. She nodded agreement. 'Fine, you start same time as Sam, quarter before seven tonight. Wear something gaudy. And now, Sam, you'd better get her out of here. Some of her admirers are drooling and I swear old Barney Hutch is wishing he were sixty again.'

'That takes care of our employment problem,' muttered Rick, while escorting her back to the hotel. 'As good a place as any other for picking up on rumours and maybe a little useful information. But now I'll tell you what I didn't have time to tell you before.'

He recounted his clash with the Kenricks and, by the time they were in Hattie's room and he lighting a cigar, had also dealt her in on a new crisis, a son of Buck Brister in custody for the murder of a farmhand and the fact that Mace Kenrick's daughter was his sweetheart.

Rick paced and smoked. Hattie sat on the edge of her bed and shook her head incredulously.

'This is something we didn't expect, Rick. The Montagues and Capulets, right here in Greco County.'

'Don't worry, I'm not completely heartless,' he quipped. 'It *could* end the feud, Martha and her Phil committing suicide, but I don't intend arranging that. Anyway, we can't be sure it'd work.'

She didn't chide him.

'You don't have to hold back the jokes, even bad jokes,' she shrugged. 'Heaven help the Braddocks if they ever lose their sense of humour. Meanwhile, the murder and the arrest won't make our task any easier.'

'We have our assignment – break up a feud,' he muttered. 'We didn't fool ourselves it'd be easy, but we didn't count on a murder. As for the Kenrick girl being in love with one of Brister's sons, I could be wrong, but I get the feeling it was a close kept secret.'

'She's loyal to her man, insists he couldn't be guilty,' mused Hattie. 'How about that? Any chance she could be right – they have the wrong man in the county jail?'

'Tough question for me to answer,' he frowned.

'This is our first day here, so it's too soon for me to play hunches. There's a lot we need to know, background on the whole dangerous situation. I have to start somewhere, so I'll look in on Red Ed now. Maybe I can get him talking.'

'What do you make of him?' asked Hattie.

'The unexpected again, big surprise,' he told her. 'The way Judy Hargrove spoke of her beloved sire, I anticipated a haunted veteran full of apprehension, unsure of himself, close to collapse. Damn it, honey, I'd hate to come to blows with him. He's tough as old saddle leather and built like a bull. Burdened by fear of this feud, apt to suffer a seizure? I'm no doctor, but I strongly doubt it. I think our Judy's a tad over-protective.'

'She *is* worried about him, so how about this?' she suggested. 'We've promised to keep in touch, let's not forget. While you're talking to her father, I could check around, find his doctor – everybody needs a doctor *sometime* – and maybe wheedle a few details about his general condition. Then I could mail off a reassuring note to the Hargroves. We've arrived and begun our investigation, and her father's in excellent health.'

'Yeah, you'd better do that,' he agreed, redonning his hat. 'And you'd better change again. Something less conspicuous. Frankly, spouse of mine, you're as much an eyeful black-haired as you are as a blonde. You're apt to stall traffic just walking along Main Street, and we don't want to give the sheriff more problems than he already has, do we?'

'What would you suggest? A false beard?'

'You don't have to go that far.'

Whitton was at his desk when Rick entered his

office. The only other party present at this time was the county jailer, Gil Keece by name, a surly individual of an age with his boss. Rick began his plea for information as diplomatically as he knew how, only to be curtly rebuffed.

'You've only just hit town,' growled Whitton. 'You're a sportin' man. I got nothin' against gamblers, but now you're makin' noises like an amateur detective, and that riles me. I got no time for any kind of amateur, Gavin.'

'I'm only asking because, like most people, I regard a feud as the worst kind of trouble for any community,' said Rick.

'And I got better to do than answer your questions,' retorted Whitton.

'If you're that all-fired curious, dude, go bother Upshaw, him that runs the newspaper,' muttered the jailer. 'He knows everything Ed gave the county attorney.'

Next stop for Rick, the offices of the Greco County *Times*.

3

How Does a Feud Begin?

A passer-by responded to Rick's request for directions. The headquarters of the county newspaper, he was told, could be found in the heart of town, north side of the main thoroughfare, corner of Main and Gersten.

On his way to his destination, Rick had to pass the Arundell General Store. A ranch wagon, its canvas inscribed Bar 9, was being loaded with supplies. Rex Abelson was standing by, rolling a cigarette. When Rick reached him, he begged a match and began a conversation.

'For a gamblin' man, you're smarter with your fists than some I've seen. Abelson's the name. I ramrod Bar 9.'

'Sam Gavin,' offered Rick, as he gave him a light. 'I hope people don't get wrong ideas about me. I don't provoke brawls. My mistake anyway. I had no way of knowing they were the girl's brothers, thought she was being seized against her will.'

'Well, she was, the way I hear it,' said Abelson. 'Big surprise. First I knew of it. Seems young Phil Brister and the Kenrick girl're sweet on each other, but they sure kept it a secret.'

'Had to, I guess,' remarked Rick. 'What choice did they have, their families locked in a feud?'

'Damn sad,' nodded Abelson. 'Sad for the whole canyon, a bad time for the smaller spreads.'

'I can understand non-combatants wouldn't want to be involved,' said Rick.

'That's how it is for my boss,' Abelson told him. 'He's a mighty worried man. Awkward for him, you know? He admires Buck Brister a lot. Same time, he's never had no trouble with the Kenricks.'

'Your boss ...' began Rick.

'His name's Prowse, Luther Prowse,' said Abelson.

'Your boss has my sympathy,' finished Rick. 'A feud's bad medicine.'

He nodded so-long and walked on to the newspaper office. Greco being a sizeable community, it didn't surprise him that the headquarters of the *Times* was big and busy. The man setting type and the one making adjustments to the printing press were in shirtsleeves and wore ink-smeared aprons. A reporter was clattering away at a Remington typewriter on a corner desk. Rick assumed the bald, bespectacled, pipe-puffing man checking copy at the main desk to be the editor. He approached him politely.

'Mister Upshaw?'

'Roger Upshaw, yeah. And you?'

'Sam Gavin. New in town. If you're not too busy ...'

'*Always* busy, mister. Comes with the job.'

'I hope you're not too busy to satisfy my curiosity.'

'About...?'

'The black cloud hanging over this territory, the Brister-Kenrick feud.'

'Read all about it in …'

'If I give you my word I'll buy your next edition, plus any earlier editions covering the subject, will you summarize all the known facts for me? Gambling is my profession, true, but I've been hired by Clint Jarrow already and, as I may become a citizen here, surely I should be as concerned as everybody else?'

'You plead quite a case, ought to be a lawyer,' grinned Upshaw. 'All right, pull up a chair and I'll tell you as much as we know about the Siddons killing.'

Having been allowed to see the statement signed by Jethro Kenrick, Upshaw was as much up to date on relevant details as the sheriff, the county attorney and as would be whichever local lawyer Buck Brister retained to defend his son.

The previous night, while taking his turn at riding guard on the Kenrick acres, the elder son had heard shooting. Clear moonlight that night, so he saw another guard, Joe Siddons, topple from his mount, also sighted a rider in cowhand's garb fleeing across Circle B range. Jethro had charged his horse across the creek, pursued, overtaken the rider and knocked him from his saddle. That rider was nineteen-year-old Phil Brister, the rancher's youngest son. One shot had been fired from his rifle.

Though Phil protested his innocence, claiming he too heard a shot while nighthawking and fired toward the gunflash, Jethro pegged him for Siddons's killer, secured him with his own lariat and brought him into town to turn him over to the sheriff.

'It looks bad for the young feller,' declared Upshaw. 'Come daylight, Deputy Schumack scouted the scene, but found no tracks of another horseman in that area. My guess is Buck Brister'll hire Horace Ingram to be defence counsel. Either that, or he'll go haywire and lead his whole outfit into town to break his boy out of the county jail.'

'Would he resort to such extremes?' asked Rick.

'Friend, the two worst hotheads in this county are Buck Brister and Mace Kenrick,' Upshaw informed him. 'So *anything's* possible.' He added, with the glee of a veteran newsman, 'And all of it'll sell papers, especially now that it's been revealed there's a love story in it. Some secret *that* must've been. I couldn't begin to guess how they ever managed to get together in private, young Phil and the Kenrick girl, but we have to believe that's what's been happening. Come to think of it, they could've been attracted to each other long before now. They were all at the county school together, the Brister and Kenrick children. Well, now that love affair's doomed and the feud can only hot up.'

'Hell of a situation,' frowned Rick.

'If you're partial to peaceful communities, you came to the wrong place at the wrong time,' said Upshaw.

'Thanks for your time,' Rick acknowledged. 'One last question?'

'Depends on the question,' said Upshaw.

'I'm guessing you've run this paper many years, so you can claim to have your finger on the pulse of Greco County,' muttered Rick.

'I don't miss much,' said Upshaw.

'So for how long have they been feuding?' demanded Rick. 'And what started it?'

The editor relit his pipe and puffed reflectively.

'Got to admit I haven't given much thought to that question. Can't tell you what started all the trouble. Up till a couple of years ago, there was peace in Greco Canyon. With their holdings separated by the creek and neither trespassing on the other, Brister and Kenrick pretty much ignored each other.'

'And then?'

'And then Kenrick accused Brister's herders of stampeding cattle across his land, trampling his crops and, next thing anybody knew, the sniping began. And, here in town, the wild brawls, farmhands and cowboys mixing it in saloons, stores and in the streets.'

'Thanks for talking to me.' Rick got to his feet. 'It's been most enlightening.'

'Thinking of trying to do something about it?' challenged Upshaw. 'Gamblers don't usually concern themselves with …'

'That's the word, sir,' declared Rick. 'Think of me as a concerned citizen.'

'That puts you in accord with the whole Greco population,' said Upshaw. 'We're all concerned. From a newspaperman's point of view, a feud is good copy, sells a lot of papers. But, like everybody else, I wish the warring factions would come to their senses and reach some kind of understanding. A truce would be mighty welcome.'

At suppertime in the hotel dining-room, the Braddocks shared a table for two, compared notes and made plans. After reporting on his parley with the *Times* editor, Rick listened to Hattie's account of her visit to one of the local doctors, Ansell Frickett no less.

For Hattie, the direct approach often paid off. The deputy to whom she had appealed for information was described as young, muscular and somewhat solemn and withdrawn, so Rick realized she couldn't be speaking of Nate Schumack. Apparently the younger deputy did not consider it a breach of confidence to inform her that, on the rare occasions that it was necessary, his boss always consulted Frickett.

'This Frickett,' she chuckled. 'Such a scrawny, irritable character.'

'Obviously you wheedled something out of him.'

'Woman's wiles, darling.'

'At that, you're the champ.'

Frickett's mood had changed for the better when his lushly beautiful visitor assured him she enjoyed good health, but believed in checking on all doctors when working a new town. A white lie transformed him from curmudgeon to gracious host; he even served a fair quality wine when she remarked a local had described him as the finest physician in the whole state of Colorado. From there on, they had socialized. On the subject of the condition of the county sheriff, Frickett had been anything but reticent.

'Strong as an ox – his exact words. He assured me Red Ed's heart is as sound as that of a twenty-one year old and that he has nerves of steel.'

'That should ease Judy's fears for her father.'

'I quoted the good doctor in the letter I wrote and mailed, as well as assuring the Hargroves we're on the job and sparing no effort to put an end to the feud.'

'Let's hope the next report we send them will be even more encouraging,' frowned Rick.

'So where do we go from here?' asked Hattie. 'Well, to the Oriental tonight, but then what?'

'I've seen nothing of the Bristers yet,' said Rick. 'Met Kenrick and his rowdy sons, also his pretty daughter, but that meeting was less than sociable and offered no opportunity for congenial conversation. I believe my next move should be to visit both parties. They aren't likely to heed an appeal for reason from a sporting man, so I'd best resort to a disguise. How about an itinerant preacher?'

'Sounds promising,' she nodded. 'A man of the cloth, and not exactly in his prime?'

'That'd be best,' he agreed. 'The Kenricks have seen me, so it'll have to be a heavy disguise, but that part's easy enough. I have a grey wig. Moustache and whiskers to match, no problem. Spectacles and a Bible – there'll be a Bible in my room I can borrow. Rusty black suit and, on our way to the Oriental, I can stop by a store and pick up a stovepipe hat.'

'I wish I could be there to see Deacon Pitch get into his act,' she smiled.

'Deacon Pitch?'

'You'll need a name, dear.'

'Sure. And Pitch'll do.'

'What'll it be? An emotional appeal – love thy neighbour – or will you hit them with the old fire and brimstone flim flam?'

'Have to size 'em up first. A good actor plays to whatever audience he finds.'

'How about the voice? I recommend that deep, sonorous baritone of yours. When you drop your voice a couple of octaves, it can be quite effective.'

'You mean loud.'

'That too.'

'I'll get directions and head for the canyon tomorrow morning,' he decided. 'No matter how I fare with the rowdy rancher and the ferocious farmer, it'll be my first chance to scout the scene of contention.' Rick added with a grimace, 'The potential battleground.'

They were on time to begin duty at the Oriental. For part of that night, Rick was in charge of the blackjack layout. Later, he took over at the roulette table. And, until 1 a.m. when the place closed, Hattie played Connie Ross to the hilt, entertaining the night-time trade with a variety of popular songs of the time, expertly accompanied by Waldo Gooch and ingratiating herself not only with the paying customers but with every member of Clint Jarrow's staff. To Rick, Jarrow predicted word of his star attraction would spread fast; he expected a record crowd next night.

Rick breakfasted early, then locked himself in his room to rig the changes. The complete transformation was achieved quickly; quick changes being the speciality of all who had worked the carny and repertory circuits.

The elderly character leaving by the window and the rear stairs bore no resemblance to the handsome young gambler now employed at the Oriental. Rick's grey wig completely concealed his dark thatch and dangled a full two inches below his shirt collar. The rumpled black suit, white shirt and black string tie were the obvious accessories, topped off by the stovepipe hat. When he descended to it, the back alley was near deserted.

Affecting a stately gait, the Bible tucked under an arm, he made his way downtown to a livery stable. He was, not for the first time, playing a role and confident that he was in character. His brows greyed, his false moustache and spade beard matching the wig, plus the steel-rimmed spectacles with unmagnified lenses, were disguise enough. This masquerade would work, he assured himself. His movements and mode of speech would complete the illusion.

At the stable, he appealed to the ostler to saddle a gentle mount for him.

'Age takes its toll, brother,' he intoned. 'Bones become weaker, muscles soften....'

'Don't I know it, Reverend,' grouched the aged stablehand. 'My rheumatic gimme a real bad time. You too, huh?

'We must all bear our crosses,' Rick said virtuously.

'Where you headed?'

'Greco Canyon, first to preach the good word to the cattlemen of Circle B, then to do likewise at the Kenrick farm. When neighbour turns against neighbour, they must be taught the virtue of charity.'

'Well, them soreheads don't listen to Red Ed nor the mayor. If you can preach some horse sense into 'em, a lotta county folks'll be beholden.'

While readying a placid-looking bay mare, the stablehand offered directions. Parallel trails led west to the canyon's mile-wide entrance. By a swing north from the creek, 'Deacon Pitch' would find himself on Circle B range. When he was through with the Bristers, he had only to return, ford the creek and head south to reach the Kenrick farm. Should he be obliged to travel at speed, Delilah was still good for a two hundred yard gallop. After that, she should be allowed to idle.

'Delilah,' Rick repeated disapprovingly, making slow work of climbing astride.

'Named by the *hombre* the boss bought her from,' recalled the stablehand. 'His name was Sid Samson and, come to think of it, he was hairless. Yup. Bald as an egg.'

Following directions, Rick easily found his way into the great canyon and on to Circle B range. Cowhands tending Buck Brister's herds paid little attention to the slow-riding man in black making for the ranch headquarters, which appeared pretty much as Rick expected. A double-storeyed home of log and clapboard, shingle-roofed like the sizeable bunkhouse. The barns were plank-roofed. There was a whole network of corrals, fifty yards separating them from the ranch-house.

As he drew closer, off-duty hands emerged from the bunkhouse. Another, toting a pitchfork, loafed out of a barn. The rancher and his elder sons appeared on the ranch-house porch after Rick reined up and boomed,

'Brother Brister, come forth!'

Buck Brister, he observed, was slightly taller than Mace Kenrick, of rangy build and craggy features, his hair greying but not receding; the typical veteran cattleman who had built his spread the hard way. Twenty-five year old Chet and his brother Dobie, three years his junior, were cast of the same mould, destined to become replicas of their sire.

Father and sons moved to the outer edge of the porch. After running an eye over the black-garbed man sitting the mare, Brister demanded, 'Just who are you and what d'you want here?'

'I am Deacon Pitch,' announced Rick.

'That makes you a son of a Pitch,' leered Dobie. Then he reeled from his father's hard slap. 'Hell, Pa...!'

'Shut your fool face,' scowled Brister.

'Harsh words, Brother Brister,' chided Rick, his deep voice audible to all. 'There have been too many harsh words in Greco Canyon, too many shots fired in anger, too much hatred! Rancour against one's neighbour avails a man naught but grief and strife!'

'This ain't a smart time to come preachin' brotherly love,' retorted Brister. 'My last born's in the calaboose for a killin' he didn't do!'

'Phil was dumb enough to take a shine to Martha Kenrick,' growled the eldest son. 'That was plenty stupid, but....'

'He wouldn't backshoot a Kenrick hand or any other man,' mumbled Dobie. 'Ain't got it in him to do a thing like that.'

'It is still to be proven,' insisted Rick. 'A jury will decide the boy's guilt or innocence. Meanwhile, Brother Brister, your son has not dishonoured you by wooing the daughter of your neighbour. I am told she is a well-raised young lady and a believer of the Lord's word.'

'She's a Kenrick!' snapped Brister. 'If you think I'd let a Kenrick marry into my family, you're outa your psalm-singin' mind! And I'm through listenin' to your palaverin'!'

'You heard the boss, Preacher,' grinned a young cowhand, drawing his six-gun. 'Now git!'

He dipped the muzzle of the weapon and cocked and fired. The bullet kicked up dust near the rented mare's left forehoof. Obviously unaccustomed to such unpleasant surprises, Delilah nickered in protest and reared. The other men expected the 'old preacher' to bite dust. But no. Rick brought the mare under control, muttered soothingly to her, then slowly dismounted, his reproachful gaze falling on the smoking Colt and its owner. As he took a step toward him, Dobie Brister sniggered and said, 'Look out, Jase. Old sin-killer's gonna clobber you.'

'Nay!' intoned Rick, still advancing. 'May the Lord restrain me from visiting physical violence on one so young and foolish!'

He reached the young cowhand. His left hand closed over the right wrist. He exerted pressure and, mouth agape and eyes popping, the waddy began buckling at the knees. Rick easily relieved him of the pistol.

'Ain't fair an old man's so strong,' the cowhand whined, massaging his wrist.

Holding the weapon with its muzzle to the ground, Rick sternly warned, 'Indiscriminate gunplay is always ill-advised. You cannot hope to anticipate the gun-skill of others. In Sioux Springs, Wyoming, two years ago, I saw a woman take first prize in the rifle shot. She was of seventy-eight years and a grandmother.' The chuck-boss had appeared, frowning inquisitively. 'Take warning, young man. Never underestimate your adversary, whatever his age.' He nodded to the chuck-boss. 'A bean can, I pray you. An empty bean can. Waste not, want not.'

The chuck-boss retreated to his kitchen and returned with the requested item. Rick gestured for him to hand it to Dobie. He obeyed. 'Deacon Pitch' then ordered Dobie to descend to the yard and hurl the can to the sky. Dobie's father and brother descended the steps, Chet declaring, 'If he can hit it once, I'll eat my hat.'

'Do it, Dobie,' grinned another man.

Dobie hurled the can high. How could he guess the visitor's real age, nor the fact that he had once earned many a useful dollar as a trick shooter?

Rick raised the Colt, took sight and started the Colt roaring, triggering fast, recocking just as fast. Gaping upward, the Bristers and the hired hands heard the pinging sounds and saw the can struck four times, each hit causing it to career back and forth. It finally came to rest over by a corral.

Lowering the weapon, Rick addressed the bug-eyed Chet. 'Do not eat your hat, boy. The Lord does not demand it, since you omitted to say "So help me God". Nor do *I* demand it.' He turned, advanced on the young cowhand and returned the gun, roughly, butting his belly with it. 'Your weapon, young man.'

'By dawg!' exclaimed the chuck-boss, first to regain the power of speech. 'If I hadn't of seen it with my own two eyes, I'd never of believed it!'

'Brother Brister!' Rick grasped the cowhand's shoulder. 'Has this brash one been properly baptized?' Before the rancher could reply, he surmised, 'Probably not. So the Lord's will be done.'

With that, he frogmarched the waddy to a horse trough and, raising him bodily, dunked him. There was a loud splash. Water slopped from the trough. He was about to ad lib a prayer when Brister yelled at him.

'You're holdin' his head down! What d'you wanta do – *drown* him?'

'Pardon?' Rick cupped hand to ear.

'I said *you're drownin' him*!' roared Brister.

'Forgive me,' sighed Rick. 'When absorbed in prayer, time means naught to me.'

'*Jase's* time's runnin' out!' gasped Chet. 'Let go of him!'

'I can perform the ceremony at a later time,' decided Rick, after which he hauled the waterlogged cowhand from the trough and let him flop to the dust, which promptly became mud. There, the waddy who'd incurred the displeasure of 'Deacon Pitch' writhed, wheezed and coughed frantically. 'I take my leave of you now, Brother Brister, praying my words will be heeded. Remember...!' He made a show of remounting old-man style. 'No good can come of hatred of one's neighbour. Brother Kenrick should be your friend ...'

'Youre loco!' blustered Brister.

'... never your enemy,' Rick continued. 'For you have much in common. You raise beef. He raises wheat, corn, barley and vegetables. What is steak without potatoes? What are vegetables without meat? I exhort you to acknowledge the error of your warlike ways and to open your heart, to let peace dwell therein. And now I go to convey the Lord's truth to Brother Kenrick.'

'All you'll get from Kenrick is buckshot in your butt!' shouted Brister, as Rick nudged the mare to a trot.

Nobody had exaggerated, he was thinking, crossing Circle B range, making south for the creek. Buck Brister was a wild one. But could he expect sweet reason from Brister at this time, his youngest son in jail on a murder charge? Well, this had been a fishing expedition. He would have had to confront the Circle B men sooner or later, assess them, sound them out. So he had done it. And now another fishing expedition. At Kenrick's, could he hope for a warmer reception? Probably not, though he doubted Kenrick, his sons or any of his hired hands would trigger buckshot at him the moment they sighted him.

Later, reaching the creek, he forded and rode a short distance south to rein up beside a clump of sizeable rocks. Delilah needed spelling. He swung down and hunkered beside her, scanning many acres of farmland, marking the contrast; from typical cattle graze he had come to the ploughed fields of an expansive farming project. Truly, the Kenricks raised fine crops. Some fields were under cultivation, all well irrigated by channels extending from the steady-flowing creek, some in full growth. No two-bit sodbuster scratching for a living was Mace Kenrick. This farm was a big, well-ordered, thriving business, and was prospering, because Kenrick knew his business.

He found a track, a wide one that could be travelled by wagons as well as riders, keeping them well clear of the fields to either side. Following that track after Delilah had rested, he came to the 18th century-style home of the Kenrick family, high gabled and built to last, and the other buildings, a barn more impressive than he'd seen at Circle B, a row of cabins, living quarters for the hired hands.

As before, his approach was noted. The hands stayed with their chores, but Kenrick's sons came striding out of the barn to curiously appraise the bewhiskered and black-clad horseman, and Kenrick himself came out to the porch of the main building followed by his daughter.

Reining up, Rick doffed his stovepipe hat to

Martha and addressed her father.

'Have I your permission, Brother Kenrick, to water my horse?'

'Go ahead,' the farmer warily invited. 'Know me, huh? Well, I don't know you. Preacher, are you?'

'I am known as Deacon Pitch,' Rick announced as he dismounted.

'We already got preachers aplenty in Greco,' frowned Orin.

'I am a wandering servant of the Lord,' explained Rick. 'My time in Greco will be brief, for there are others, folk of smaller towns far from here, in need of spiritual counsel. I travel where my ministry takes me.'

'Take care of his horse, Orin,' ordered Kenrick. 'Now tell me, Deacon Pitch, what brings you here?'

'The friction,' Rick said sombrely. 'The rivalry – a feud pitting brother against brother …'

'We ain't kin to them Bristers,' growled Jethro.

'Brothers in the eyes of the Lord,' declared Rick. 'I have appealed to the Bristers. I now appeal to your father.'

'Look, Deacon, there's nothin' you can say that'll change anything,' warned Kenrick. 'It's 'tween us and the Bristers and no business of no driftin' preacher. Brister's youngest shot Joe Siddons and justice is gonna be done.'

'Please, Pa …' began Martha.

'Hold your tongue,' he chided.

'The slaying of your employee was a vile deed and tragic,' conceded Rick. 'If the boy charged with the murder is indeed guilty …'

'What d'you mean – if?' challenged Jethro. 'I ain't blind. I know what I saw.'

'And what *did* you see, son?' demanded Rick.

'Brother Siddons slain by the Brister boy before your very eyes? Nay! You saw him fleeing and assumed him to be the murderer. Does he not protest his innocence?'

'That no-good whelp'd never admit it,' jeered Kenrick.

'Why should he admit to something he'd never do?' cried Martha. 'Phil is kind. He's a decent person.'

'You keep bendin' my ear about him and I'll tan your hide,' her father threatened.

'Control your evil temper!' boomed Rick, and placed a protective hand on the girl's shoulder. 'Heed me, Brother Kenrick. Should the boy be proven innocent of this terrible crime, it may be the Lord's will that he should become your son-in-law.'

'Over our dead bodies,' scowled Jethro.

'Don't preachers ever *think*?' The farmer wanted to know. 'Put yourself in my place, Deacon. Try to savvy how *you'd* feel. For who knows how long, my last born's been foolin' with Brister's last born behind my back – betrayin' her family!'

'Answer me truthfully, child,' urged Rick, and turned the girl to match his gaze. 'Have you cause for shame? You met Philip Brister in secret?' She nodded and winced. 'Did you encourage him to take advantage – did you sin?'

'It was nothing like that!' She shook her head emphatically. 'We just met when we could and – and talked of what we feel for each other – but we didn't *do* anything. We love each other, but he never wanted me to – to give myself to him. We want to be married. I'm not ashamed and – Phil doesn't need to be ashamed either. And that's the gospel truth.'

'Take heart, child,' soothed Rick. 'Have faith. Do not despair.' He took his hand from her shoulder and looked at the brothers. Orin had watered the mare and was eyeing him sullenly, his lips still puffy. Jethro's nose was still bruised. 'You young men have suffered injury. I will pray your pain may be eased.'

'Pray all you want,' muttered Kenrick. 'But don't poke your snoot into what's none of your business.'

'Pa!' frowned Martha.

'Be not distressed, child,' sighed Rick. 'Your father speaks in anger, but I forgive him.' He took the mare's rein from Orin. 'Thank you, my son.' Then, before raising boot to stirrup, he offered advice to the farmer. 'Your daughter has denied any wrong-doing in her relationship with the boy she loves. I believe her. You should believe her. A girl who values her chastity merits the trust of her parent. Meditate on that thought, Brother Kenrick, I beg you.'

He had, he decided, said as much as he could think of to the Kenricks. Best not overplay it. Best make his exit while he was ahead.

Ahead? Riding for the canyon entrance, he realized he was by no means ahead of the game. How much had he achieved? Not a great deal, beyond accurately pegging the Bristers to be as bellicose, as mule-headed as the Kenricks. Nevertheless, he had familiarized himself with the area of conflict, which could prove useful.

One aspect of the whole sorry business intrigued him. He had to conclude the Kenrick girl was of her late mother's temperament. Certainly, she was gentler than her father and hard-nosed brothers. The same applied to Phil Brister, he supposed. He could not imagine Martha falling in love with Chet or Dobie Brister, both of them too uncouth for such a refined young lady. So Martha and her Phil had to be two of a kind, peace-loving and no doubt frustrated by the animosity between their families.

Had Phil Brister triggered that lethal bullet? Interesting question. Why hadn't it occurred to him before? It threw a new light on the case. If, as the boy claimed, he had seen the flash of the gun that had ended Joe Siddons's life and been thwarted in his pursuit of that party by Jethro Kenrick, who *had* killed Siddons – and why?

He skirted cactus and spruce *en route* to the canyon entrance and continued his homeward journey with another, more immediate thought pestering him. When he reached the county seat, he would need to move with care. Deacon Pitch had to disappear before Sam Gavin reappeared.

Back in town, he returned the mare and paid for its rental. He trudged the northside alley toward the rear of the Hubbard Hotel, the Bible tucked under an arm, his wary eyes on locals out and about. Nobody was looking his way when he reached the steps leading up to the rear gallery. He climbed them to find his wife taking her ease, perched on the windowsill of her room, buffing her nails. In her black wig and bright red gown, she would have been visible for miles.

'Well, howdy, handsome.'

She drawled that greeting as he passed her, adding an artful wink.

'Shameless hussy,' he growled in his preacher's accents.

He moved on to enter his room by way of his window and, moments later, she was climbing in to join him.

4

Find the Motive

Hattie closed the window, lowered the shade, made herself comfortable and, while her husband removed his disguise, demanded to be told the outcome of his visits to the rival camps. He offered his theory about the young lovers being unfortunate enough to have inherited their mothers' genes and personalities, a couple of innocents caught between a rock and a hard place.

'The Romeo and Juliet of Greco County,' she agreed. 'I guess, being detectives, we're supposed to be hard-boiled. Are we?'

'You know the answer to that question,' he muttered. 'I've only met the girl. You've met neither of them, but we aren't *that* hard-boiled. You pity them as much as I do.'

'We're a couple of incurable romantics. Even so, we'd best not forget Judy Hargrove's daddy is our assignment.'

'This feud's our assignment. Red Ed'll be a happier man when it's over and done with, but so will a lot of other people, especially Romeo and Juliet. If the boy's innocence can be established, their surly sires may become sadder and wiser men, and maybe more receptive to the prospect of their being joined in holy wedlock.'

'Right. We Braddocks have always loved happy endings. That's where we differ with Billy The Bard. Too many of his plays had miserable, gory endings. So, husband mine, where do we go from here?'

'Had your lunch yet?'

'Waited for you. And it's that time. I'm hungry.'

'Fine. You go on down. Maybe you can claim that same corner table for us. Be with you in ten minutes.'

'Sure you'll be smooth-faced? Spirit gum sticks, as if we didn't know. I have ample cold cream if you're running short.'

'No, I have all I need. Say farewell to the preacher. Sam Gavin'll join you in a little while.'

'I'm glad you're through with that stovepipe hat,' Hattie remarked as she moved to the window. 'On Abe Lincoln, that kind of tile looked just right. But on you? Never, dearest. Not your style. Not even with the grey wig, the rusty suit and the chin whiskers.'

Rick had a raging appetite and a lot on his mind when, rigged again as Sam Gavin, he descended to the dining-room to take lunch with his wife. For a while, he concentrated on accounting for much needed nourishment. Then he began talking again, quietly, pensively, to a beautiful audience of one.

'I believe young Brister. Jumpy Jethro saw no third party so, as far as he was concerned, it had to be Phil put that bullet in the farmhand's back.'

'If you're right,' frowned Hattie, 'we have a

mystery here. Who'd have a motive? I got to talking with that hefty young deputy while you were gone. Chris Dewkes?'

'You visited the sheriff's office?' asked Rick.

'I was nowhere near Daddy Whitton's office. Needed some air, took a stroll and where do you suppose I found Deputy Dewkes? Loitering by the schoolyard fence. The future taxpayers of this fair city were taking their mid-morning break, playing tag, throwing a ball around – you know how kids are.'

'Sure. Used to be a kid myself.'

'Were you an adorable little boy or a repulsive brat? It's something I've often wondered about.'

'Make your point.'

'Well, I saw Min again. Minerva Platt, the new schoolma'am who talked with us on our way here?'

'I remember her. So?'

'She was doing her duty, keeping an eye on the children. But not Deputy Dewkes. He had eyes only for her. Maybe he's smitten. Well, I distracted him a little, drew him into conversation. I like him, Rick. Ask him a question, any question, he'll give you as clear an answer as he can manage.'

'And what was your question?'

'I asked him if he'd been acquainted with the murder victim and just what kind of man Joe Siddons was.'

'I'm glad you did. It could be relevant. What'd he have to say about Siddons?'

'He knew him quite well. And liked him. If we're to believe my informant, Siddons was a genial soul, easy-going, a typical farmhand and – he stressed this – too good-natured to have enemies.'

While they were lingering over their coffee, Rick

pondered the Siddons shooting and began speculating.

'The Bristers are enemies of the whole Kenrick crew,' he mused. 'But it seems pointless, doesn't it, a Brister rider backshooting Siddons?'

'Taking harassment too far,' was Hattie's opinion. 'Going to unnecessary extremes, no matter how antagonistic they are.'

'And it's not as if Siddons had forded the creek and was trespassing on Circle B land,' said Rick. 'So what about the shot Phil Brister heard? His claim is that he saw the gun-flash while riding nighthawk, fired in that direction and tried to pursue the other man, but was headed off by Jethro Kenrick.'

'If we believe the Brister boy ...' began Hattie.

'Uh huh,' he grunted. 'Two possibilities. A Circle B rider shot Siddons just for the hell of it. Phil's arrest must have shaken him, but he's keeping his mouth shut, protecting his own neck.'

'The other possibility?' demanded Hattie.

'A third party involved,' frowned Rick. 'I'm not forgetting the deputy's opinion of Siddons. Too good-natured to have enemies. On the other hand, whoever put that bullet in him was certainly no friend of his.'

'So....' She shrugged helplessly. 'We all make enemies, like it or not, intentionally or unwittingly.'

'The whole thing is getting complicated,' he complained. 'And I hate complications.'

'Listen to who's talking,' she teased. 'Every case we've worked had a plot cluttered with inconsistencies and red herrings. Think of the Shay City fracas. Think of our tour with the Ella Cardew company. Detective work has never been easy for us. And we've had some close calls, lover. But you always cut through the complications and we always win out.'

'Don't give me all the credit,' he said. 'You're one hell of a partner when the chips're down and the going gets rough.'

Lunch over, they left the dining-room and, for a while, shared a sofa in the lobby. Hattie, the epitome of wifely loyalty, offered encouragement, urging Rick to recall everything he had learned of the Brister-Kenrick feud, thus reminding him of his parley with the *Times* editor.

'How it all started,' he reflected. 'Cattle trampling a field of wheat ready for harvesting. It happened at night and Kenrick automatically accused Circle B. Came then the sniping and, any time Brister and Kenrick men were in town, the fighting.'

'Could Kenrick positively identify those stampeding beeves as Circle B stock?' wondered Hattie. 'Probably not. If, for instance, it happened on a dark night, how could any farmhand see the brands? We know Kenrick men traded shots with snipers north of the creek. Those snipers could have been Circle B hands, but are we certain?'

'Can Kenrick be certain?' That was Rick's next thought. 'And would Brister know for sure his nighthawks were snap-shooting at farmhands? We're talking about a lot of land. Kenrick owns a large acreage. Brister's range extends even farther.'

'To win answers to those questions, you'd have to play preacher again, ride to the canyon and talk to the mulish rivals,' said Hattie. 'And I doubt Deacon Pitch is eager to give a second performance.'

'The whole hullabaloo *could* have been triggered

by a third party for whatever his reasons,' declared Rick. 'We'll stick with that hunch a while and see where it leads us. Meanwhile, I'd better spend most of this afternoon on my back, get as much sleep as possible before we go to work tonight.'

'Planning a little nocturnal action?'

'After the saloon closes, I'll change, rent a horse and take a ride to the canyon again. This time, I'll stake out. It could all be for nothing but, if I'm lucky, if there's more shooting, I might do better than Phil Brister.'

'Shoot the sniper.'

'Better than that. Tag him. And, if he doesn't flee to the Circle B headquarters, it won't be a hunch any more. we'll know somebody else has taken a hand in the game. Upshaw said Kenrick and Brister seemed to be cohabiting peacefully enough up till a couple of years ago. That's when the trouble began.'

'Now it gets *very* interesting,' enthused Hattie. 'If neither Kenrick nor Brister made the first hostile move, who did?'

'That's the big question,' nodded Rick. 'And, if I can find an answer to it, we'll get our chance to earn what Judy's well-heeled husband's paying us – plus that fat bonus.'

Until five o'clock that afternoon, he adhered to tried and true Braddock logic. A man is not a machine. Deprived of adequate sleep, a detective cannot hope to function efficiently, all reflexes sharp, the mind clear, the constitution ready for anything.

Shaving and bathing refreshed him. He donned grey striped pants, a fresh white shirt, brightly-patterned cravat, silk-faced vest and black frock coat and, with his gaudily-gowned wife, downed a hearty supper before leaving for the Oriental.

Clint Jarrow's prediction proved accurate. A bigger than average crowd, the games of chance well patronized and the barkeeps kept busy, thanks to the establishment's new attraction. Hattie now enjoyed a rapport with the obliging Waldo Gooch, who backed her with gusto as she entertained the crowd. Plenty of variety. Sentimental ballads loved by all, plus cheerful ditties that had farmboys and ranch-hands tapping in time and applauding gleefully.

On duty at the roulette layout, Rick was able to dart quick glances at all parties present. He, and also the observant Jarrow, anticipated there could be trouble. Both Kenrick brothers were here, also more than a few cowhands, some of whom had ridden to town on horses wearing the Circle B brand.

Jarrow wasn't waiting for trouble to start. He took the initiative after Hattie finished her tenth song. When the applause subsided, he raised his voice, but not aggressively, just loud enough for all to hear.

'I want no trouble here tonight. Enjoy yourselves, boys, but keep it peaceful, understand?'

This drew a growled rejoinder from the stoop-shouldered cattleman nursing a shot of rye with an elbow propped on the bar. He was Jesse Vance, the Circle B foreman.

'Won't be no trouble, Jarrow. Not 'less the Kenricks start it, the way they started the feud by takin' pot shots at Circle B night herders.'

Orin Kenrick was promptly on his feet, fists clenched.

'No Kenrick or any of our hired hands fired them first shots!' he cried.

'Easy, gents.' Rick paid a winner and supported Jarrow's demand. 'Keep your arguments in Greco Canyon. This saloon's your place of entertainment, not a battleground.'

'Him again.' The elder brother recognized Rick and scowled at him. 'The dude that punches sneaky.'

'We ain't through with you yet, tinhorn,' warned Orin.

'Anything you want to settle, choose another time,' advised Rick. 'And another place – anywhere else but here.'

'Jarrow, I'll keep my bunch in line,' offered Vance. 'The ploughboys're your problem.'

'Place your bets, gents.' Rick returned his attention to his clients. 'The wheel turns, the white pill bounces on its merry way and who knows who the next winner will be?'

Hattie made it a short break. She nodded to Waldo, who vamped an introduction to launch her into another lively song. The tension eased. Farmhands who'd travelled in with their boss's sons listened to the singing for another hour before leaving. Discretion was the better part of their valour at this time; there were more cowmen than farmboys in the Oriental tonight.

Around eleven o'clock, Hattie took another break during which, covertly observed by her husband, she joined the Circle B ramrod at the bar to sip a cup of coffee and socialize with him. Rick wasn't worrying. Reading Hattie's mind in fact. Jesse Vance must have been otherwise engaged during "Deacon Pitch's" visit to the ranch headquarters. He hadn't seen the man before. So he, like all other potential combatants, should be sized up, and Hattie was doing just that.

It was a profitable night for Clint Jarrow, the gambling supervisors staying as busy as the bartenders, the record crowd demanding encore after encore from "Connie Ross" who, fortunately, was a tireless entertainer. Nevertheless, this was a mid-week night and all customers remembering business is business and jobs are jobs. Tomorrow would be another working day for men obliged to rise early. And so, by 12.45 a.m., the saloon began emptying. Townmen and ranch-hands retreated from the games of chance.

Jarrow and his staff were ready to call it a day. The only drinkers remaining were the Kenrick brothers, who had to be asked to leave. By now, they were flushed and near incoherent from an excessive intake of cheer.

'What the hell?' Jethro mumbled as he and his brother lurched toward the batwings. 'Tanner's Bar'll still be open.'

'Sure enough,' agreed Orin, and hiccupped. 'And Tanner's booze's as good as we been drinkin' here.'

Before escorting his wife to their hotel, Rick had to wait for Jarrow and every member of his staff to finish complimenting her. She was good for business. None of them expected Connie Ross and her gentleman friend would stay in Greco indefinitely and, when they decided to try their luck elsewhere, they would be sorely missed. Meanwhile, they had made themselves very popular, especially the black-haired singer in the bright green gown.

When they finally departed, Hattie linked arms with her husband and remarked, 'If those Kenrick brothers rise at dawn, it'll be a painful awakening. Either the feud has driven them to drink or they live in fear the distilleries will ban deliveries to this town.'

'Not the smartest farmboys I've ever known,' was Rick's comment. 'As proddy as the Circle B crew I'd say. And that's my cue for a question. What'd you make of that Vance jasper?'

'Everything a good ranch foreman ought to be,' she shrugged. 'Loyal to his boss and the whole outfit. But I got an impression.'

'Here we go again. Woman's intuition.'

'Jesse Vance'll handle his share of the fighting if the dispute explodes into all-out war, but he won't enjoy it.'

'A tough veteran who, given a choice, would prefer an outbreak of peace – that's your impression?'

'Strong impression. Most of the time we were talking, he tended to reminisce – wistfully it seemed to me – about the good years. That's what he called the period before the feud began. The good years when ranch-hands tended the herds and farmhands ploughed and sowed and harvested. Neighbourly was how he recalled that time. Apparently it was all very friendly. From both sides of the creek, Kenrick and Brister hands would often wave to one another.'

'And now they trade shots and it's gotten out of hand. Siddons was buried today and every Kenrick's temper is on a short fuse.'

'But, if Siddons wasn't killed by a Brister rider ...'

'If I can prove it, honey, we may still prevent a blood-bath, so I'm riding out to the canyon now.'

'To watch and wait?'

'Just in case.'

In the lobby, they collected their keys and climbed to their rooms. Outside Rick's door, Hattie kissed him, delivered a brief speech on the subject of self-protection. As well, she had a question.

'Would Judy's father approve of this little scouting expedition?'

'He mustn't know,' was Rick's prompt reply. 'The fact is Sheriff Whitton doesn't like me.'

'That's hard to believe,' she said fondly. 'Anybody – anywhere – disliking my darling Rick.'

'Doesn't like me,' Rick stressed. 'Doesn't approve of me. He made that clear enough, believe me. Called me an amateur and named amateurs as his pet aversion. It doesn't bother me and I still respect the man, but he'd better not know I'm on the case till we've solved it. So the rule is, till it's all over, what Red Ed doesn't know won't hurt him – nor us.'

'I'll see you in the morning?'

'Don't count on our having breakfast together. I have no way of guessing when I'll be back.'

In his own room, while Hattie was retiring in hers, he changed to garb more suited for his purpose, Levis, a wool shirt, a hip-length denim jacket. He re-secured his shoulder holstered .38 which would be concealed by the jacket, strapped on his Colt, donned his Stetson and was ready.

He went to a different livery stable to rent a saddle-animal and his choice was a strong-limbed chestnut gelding. Then he was quitting town and headed for the canyon in clear moonlight, scanning the sky and wondering how long the moonlight would prevail; seeking a stakeout position in pitch dark could be irritating and time-wasting.

Once, glancing over his shoulder, he sighted two other riders a good distance to his rear, also bound for the canyon. He reined up a moment. The wind was blowing from the east, so the hoofbeats were audible. And other sounds. An inane guffaw and a tinkling of breaking glass. The Kenrick brothers certainly had continued their drinking spree, even buying a bottle for their homeward journey, empty now and tossed away to smash against a rock.

He rode on to the canyon entrance, swung northward on to Circle B range and, across soft grass, his horse's hoofbeats muffled, made for a small copse. Reaching it, he swung down, tied the animal and hunkered by the west edge of the trees to begin his vigil.

Farther away across the range, a steer or two lowed. He heard the far-off wail of a coyote while his gaze switched to the creek and the rock cluster and, beyond, the fields of the Kenrick farm. A sack of Bull Durham and a box of matches had been stowed in a pocket of his jacket. He craved a smoke, but gave no thought to rolling one. The brief flare of a match could tip his hand if spotted by other parties.

Other parties. He wondered about that and pondered his theory again. Somebody else, whose motive was anybody's guess, *could* have committed the murder for which Phil Brister had been charged.

Cling to that thought, boy, he urged himself. It could be the answer you need – and could there be a better way to settle this conflict?

He waited almost an hour. It took that long for the Kenrick brothers, too drunk to dare kicking their mounts to speed, to reach the canyon. Rick changed position to watch them ford the creek. And then, just as they reached the south bank, it happened.

The shot was triggered from Circle B range somewhere west of Rick's stakeout; of that he was sure. He saw Orin Kenrick pitch from his horse and at once retreated to untie and mount the chestnut. As he did so, he heard, farther along the creek, the splashing sound of another rider making the crossing. Out of the copse he charged to hustle his mount across the creek and approach the brothers.

Orin was prone and groaning, Jethro making slow work of dismounting, but with his head clearing a little. Shock did tend to sober a man. Arriving, Rick swung down and crouched beside the shooting victim.

'What the hell…?' began Jethro.

'I'll tell you this much, if you think your mind can take it all in …' began Rick.

'You're that smart-ass dude tinhorn. What're you doin'?'

'Use your eyes. I'm taking a look at your brother's wound. Now listen to me. He was shot from the north side of the creek but, if a Circle B man did the shooting, why'd he ford to this side right afterward?'

'You sure he…?'

'Dead sure. Heard him clearly. Now lend a hand here. We have to raise Orin to a sitting position.'

'Aw, hell, I'm hurtin' bad!' groaned Orin. 'I'm gonna die for sure!'

'Not from this wound, sonny,' muttered Rick, as he began stripping him of his upper garments. 'The way the bullet tore your clothes – didn't make a hole – suggests it creased you. Scratch a match, Jethro, hold it close.' He untied his bandanna and swabbed blood from either side of the gash. 'Uh huh. Not too deep, Knot your bandanna and Orin's together. You boys favour sizeable neckerchiefs. I'll hold mine to the wound while you run the makeshift bandage around him. Not that way, Jethro. You have to knot it on the *other* side.'

'Doin' the best I can,' mumbled Jethro.

'Do you have enough length, can you tie it?'

'Tyin' it now.'

'Fine, help me get his clothes back on. Orin, you feel strong enough to sit your horse? You only have to hold on to the saddlehorn. Jethro will lead. I'll be right beside you to steady you.'

'We're too far from town!' cried Orin. 'I'd leak all my blood 'fore we could reach a doc!'

'We're taking you home,' said Rick. 'What do you say, Jethro? Does anybody at the farm know enough to help him?'

'Martha,' growled Jethro. 'She dunno how to pick the right man for herself, but she ain't forgot nothin' Ma learned her 'bout doctorin' a hurt.'

'Here we go, Orin,' said Rick.

They lifted the younger brother astride his horse. Rick got a grip on his pants-belt. Orin at once grasped his saddlehorn and hung on for dear life, much as though he'd fallen over a cliff and grasped an outjutting rock. When Jethro remounted and took the rein of his brother's animal, Rick swung astride the chestnut.

'Can't go fast,' Jethro warned as they started the

horses moving.

'Shortest route to the farmhouse, but slowly,' nodded Rick. 'Easy does it.'

They had travelled only a hundred yards before a rider intercepted them, a farmhand armed with a rifle.

'They did it again, the sonsabitches!' he raged. 'This time, they got Orin!'

'Keep patrollin', Clem, and be real careful,' ordered Jethro.

As they rode on, Rick was mentally rehearsing a speech; there were things he intended discussing with Mace Kenrick and, under these circumstances, he thought it likely Kenrick would have to give him a hearing – and some thought to what he had to say.

Jethro bellowed to arouse his father and sister when they were in sight of the family home. Lamplight shone from several windows by the time they were reining up. First to dismount, Rick muttered orders.

'Leave your brother to me. I'll carry him in. Be ready to lead me to wherever his wound is to be treated.'

'Kitchen table,' said Jethro.

'Wherever,' shrugged Rick, and positioned himself beside Orin's horse. 'All right, son, you can let go now. Just swing your leg over. If you're feeling weak, don't worry, you won't hit the ground. I'm right here.'

When the door opened and light shafted onto the porch, Jethro had tied the three horses and Rick was toting the younger brother in his arms. Kenrick and his daughter, robes covering their sleeping clothes, emerged, calling questions anxiously. Jethro, though hungover, was able to offer a fairly coherent explanation; he then moved in to clear the table in the kitchen.

'You...?' the farmer began as Rick carried Orin to the porch.

'Happened to be in the neighbourhood, sir,' said Rick. 'We bound the gash as best we could. Miss Martha – nice to see you again – I'd suggest warm water and the best soap you have.'

'And iodine,' she decided.

'Iodine!' wailed Orin.

'Flesh wound,' Rick informed Kenrick while toting his burden into the kitchen. 'Not too deep, but he lost blood. I'm no doctor, but I believe he'll need to rest a few days and take plenty of nourishment.'

Martha busied herself at the stove. After depositing Orin on the table, Rick waited for the farmer to finish berating his sons. They had stayed in town too late. They had disobeyed his orders by indulging in a drinking jag. A man befuddled by booze is wide open to attack. They were old enough to know better, etc.

When Kenrick paused to catch his breath, Jethro said his piece.

'The gamblin' man forded and – uh – helped all he could. Showed up real fast, only it wasn't him creased Orin. It was a rifle shot for sure, and he don't tote no rifle.'

'Thanks for clearing that up,' said Rick. 'And the gambling man has a name. Gavin. Sam Gavin.'

'How come you ain't duded up like the first time we saw you?' demanded Kenrick.

'I had my reasons for hiding on Circle B land,' said Rick. 'We'll talk of that later. May I help, Miss Martha?'

'I'd be obliged, Mister Gavin,' she nodded. 'Orin's apt to struggle when I swab that gash.'

The girl, after heating water, worked deftly, exposing the wound by ridding her brother's left side of congealed blood. Orin would have writhed and kicked, had Rick not held him down by his shoulders and Jethro by his legs. Kenrick responded to her gentle request, retreating to the main bedroom to fetch clean bandaging, iodine and ointment. For some time thereafter, the patient made himself heard, and then some; plainly, pain and Orin Kenrick were arch enemies.

He was hoarse by the time his sister had applied a dressing and secured it with a bandage wound round his torso.

'I have his shoulders,' Rick reminded everybody. 'Jethro, take his legs again. Miss Martha, if you'll precede us to his bed.' While the younger son was being bedded down, he made Kenrick an offer. 'I could send a doctor out here as soon as I return to town, if you wish.'

'No, he'll heal,' declared Kenrick. 'The way the girl took care of him, ain't no danger of blood poisonin'. She'll keep checkin' his wound till he's fit for his chores again.'

When they returned to the kitchen, Rick remarked, 'It occurs to me this is my first chance to apologize to you good folk. Our first meeting, the run-in outside the sheriff's office. There is, of course, a simple explanation which I hope you'll accept. I had just arrived in Greco. Seeing two men leap from a wagon and seize Miss Martha, I thought I was witnessing an abduction.'

'Yes, you thought you were rescuing me,' frowned Martha. 'Be reasonable, Pa. How must it have looked to Mister Gavin?'

'Just like he says, I guess,' Kenrick grudgingly conceded.

'No hard feelings, Jethro?' asked Rick.

'Well – I reckon not,' shrugged Jethro.

'You young folk should turn in now,' Rick suggested. 'Mister Kenrick, your sleep was broken. But, if you can spare a little more time, we should talk.'

Martha and her elder brother withdrew. Kenrick followed Rick out to the porch, watched him perch on the rail and fish out his makings and sank into a chair.

'All right, Gavin,' he said. 'You helped fetch Orin home and you're actin' real polite, so I'll allow you're entitled to my time.'

'We can talk about this calmly and reasonably – or get into an argument which wouldn't help either of us,' declared Rick.

'Depends what you want to talk about,' Kenrick said guardedly.

Rick finished building a smoke, touched a flaring match to it and took a drag.

'Phil Brister can't be blamed for this shooting,' he pointed out.

'He's in jail where he oughta be. So one of his brothers, or any Circle B man.'

'Mister Kenrick, I don't believe any of Brister's men wounded Orin.'

'You can believe what you ...'

'I don't believe it, because I heard a rider cross the creek right after I heard the shot. Why would a Circle B man do that? More likely he'd stay on home range or head back to the bunkhouse.'

'He forded to this side to throw you off his track.'

'I'm certain he didn't know I was there. I arrived quietly and hid in a copse. I was there quite a time before your sons arrived.'

'So what're you tryin' to say?'

'I have to answer your question with a question, and the question is – do you know anybody who wants you and your family out of Greco Canyon?'

'You mean – pull up stakes, quit my farm that I own, the land we've ploughed and seeded and harvested for years?'

'I wondered if anybody had made you an offer, tried to buy you out.'

'Nobody ever did. Look, I don't savvy why a gambler'd give a damn about what's happenin' in the canyon, but I'll tell you this for nothin'. The only man makin' trouble for us, the only one wants rid of us Kenricks, is Buck Brister – with his sons and his hired gunhawks backin' him.'

'Had you ever quarrelled? Was there any ill feeling between you before...?'

'Before his herders stampeded cattle 'cross my land, tramplin' crops? No. Before that, we were just neighbours. I made no trouble for him, he made none for me.'

'I'm told it happened at night. A night like this?'

'No. Dark. No moonlight.'

'Yet you're sure they were Circle B cattle?'

'Had to be. It was only a couple nights later they started shootin' at my night guards. So, by damn, my boys shot right back at 'em.' The farmer leaned forward in his chair. 'I ain't stupid, Gavin. To me, it's plain enough Brister got greedy a couple years back and started cravin' my land, more land for his cattle, so he could spread himself, raise bigger herds.'

'Well, sir.' Rick shrugged helplessly and slid from the porch-rail. 'I won't trade harsh words with you. Besides, you need your sleep. We may talk again at some later time.'

'Somethin' about you don't make a lick o' sense to me,' complained Kenrick. 'What've you got to win by buttin' into this ruckus? You're a sportin' man, likely the wanderin' kind. So why should you care a hoot in hell what happens here?'

'I don't like feuds, that's all,' said Rick. 'Come to think of it, that's putting it mildly. I *hate* feuds – and what they do to people. Lives in danger, the threat of bloodshed and suffering, I hate all that. You asked a fair question. I gave you a fair answer. Let's leave it at that for the present, Mister Kenrick. The hour is late. We need our sleep.' He turned to the steps. 'Goodnight to you.' Pausing, he checked his watch. 'Should've said good morning.'

He untied the chestnut, mounted and headed back toward the creek. In a matter of moments, the Kenrick home would be in darkness again, the farmer assuming the concerned newcomer was on his way back to the county seat.

But the concerned newcomer had other ideas.

Upon reaching the near bank of Greco Creek, Rick wheeled his horse and began following it westward. He knew what he was looking for; there would still be sign to be read. No rain had fallen on this territory since his and Hattie's arrival, so the ground could still be damp, meaning that part of the bank at which the rifleman who'd made an attempt on Orin Kenrick's life had finished his fording of the creek.

5

Frightened Lady

Three times, Rick paused and dismounted to run the palms of his hands over grass close to the bank. While doing this, he gave thanks for his decision to spend most of the previous afternoon flat on his back in a comfortable bed. He was not yet weary, mentally or physically.

The fourth time he checked, he found what he sought. Out of his saddle, he scanned the terrain both sides of the creek and decided to take a chance. The match flared briefly, just long enough for him to spot the fresh hoof tracks. Dropping to his knees, he felt at the grass. Drying, but still a hint of dampness. Yes, this section of the creek was far enough from his own fording place to be the place at which the sniper had crossed.

He remounted after satisfying himself that, from here, the rider had proceeded south-west. The chestnut was kept to a slow walk for a considerable distance, after which the wind changed and he caught a whiff of cattle.

Untended cattle, he discovered some time later. No cloud-banks obscured the moon. He had the steers under observation when he dismounted. Leaving the horse ground-reined inside a patch of brush, he trudged slowly to the nearest steer. It shifted slightly, but did not take fright. Reaching it, he studied its brand.

He was deep in thought when he returned to the brush to remount and head eastward.

Questions clamoured in his brain. Did the sniper have to be a Bar 9 man? Maybe not. Certainly his tracks led to Bar 9 range, but only for as far as Rick had tagged them. The rider could have circled the herd and ridden onward. Somewhere farther west, he could have crossed the creek again. Anything was possible.

What did he know of Bar 9? So far, the only associate of Luther Prowse he had met was his foreman, Rex Abelson, and Abelson had seemed a normal, reasonable, honest enough man.

On the other hand, think of other seemingly normal, honest enough men you've encountered, he invited himself.

Ah, memories. In his late teens, after he had turned prospector, he recalled pausing on the trail leading to his lonely claim in the Sierra Nevada. A rider coming from the opposite direction, a smiling, genial type, halted him to beg a light. He had lit the man's cigar, offered him some extra matches and, for a few minutes, they had traded pleasantries. After friendly farewells, they had separated, Rick continuing on his way. But some instinct had compelled him to glance over his shoulder. That so genial fellow was aiming a gun at him, would have snuffed out his life for his horse, the clothes on his back and the supplies he was fetching back from a trading post. Rick drew first, put his bullet in the man's shoulder, secured him to his horse and delivered him to the nearest sheriff's office.

A poker party in a Utah saloon three years later. The most amiable, open-faced man he had met in a long time was seated opposite him and winning pot after pot, till he detected his sharping technique, a high card slipped from his sleeve. That lowdown trickery had cost the sharper a front tooth and a broken nose, also his ill-gotten winnings.

Flagstaff, Arizona. It would have been only two years later. On a busy street, he had been jostled by a harmless-looking, well-dressed man who apologized profusely. Rick had accepted the apology, but not the deft purloining of his wallet. And indicated his displeasure by retrieving same and kicking the thief twelve yards to a water trough and into it, face-down.

You couldn't judge a book by its cover. It was just as true, he knew from experience, that a pleasing exterior could camouflage larcenous, sometimes homicidal instincts.

So working on the assumption that the sniper was a Bar 9 man, did he have his own axe to grind or was he under his boss's orders; was Luther Prowse the brain behind the feud, the schemer who had triggered all the animosity between the Bristers and Kenricks? If so, why? What was Prowse's motive?

Tough questions and, no use fooling himself, he was tiring now, had done much during the after midnight hours. As he approached the part of the creek separating farmland from Circle B range, the sun took its cue and made its entrance, rising slowly over the horizon far east of the county seat.

First light arrived. Nearing the rock cluster on Kenrick land, he stifled a yawn and decided to water the chestnut before continuing on his way; also he craved the comfort of tobacco again.

He dismounted and, after letting the horse slake its thirst, cupped his hands and did the same for himself. Then, leading the animal to the rocks, he left it ground-reined, fished out his Bull Durham and moved closer to the rock clump.

It was a natural posture. Prop a shoulder against a rock, a plank wall, a lamp-post, any kind of post, while building a smoke. Nine out of ten men did it. There were no walls, no posts of any kind hereabouts, so he just happened to put his weight against part of a rock – and never did get around to rolling that cigarette.

The pressure of his shoulder dislodged it – just like that – a ten by twelve inch part of the rock. It fell and, off-balance, so did he, spilling tobacco and the cigarette paper, sprawling.

He swore wearily as he began picking himself up. On his feet again, he was perplexed. The boulders clustered here had appeared solid, not the type to so easily give way under pressure. To chip out that one chunk, one would normally have to use a pickaxe, not to mention considerable force. Only natural he was weary at this time, and he didn't resent it. What he resented was being both weary and perplexed; not his idea of a happy state of mind.

Retrieving his Durham, he found the sack contained just enough for one cigarette and managed to rescue one cigarette paper from the dawn breeze before the others were carried away. A quirley was rolled and lit. He smoked for a moment and glanced at the indentation caused by dislodgement of that piece of rock.

And the hair on his neck tingled.

At first he was incredulous. But then, having prospected in earlier years, he had to acknowledge what he was seeing. A streak that gleamed. A vein. A pay vein. Gold. With his pulse quickening, he bent to pick up the chunk he had shoved loose and turned it over to inspect its inner side. The same sign, and matching the other. Slowly, very carefully, he fitted it back into its former position. The line of the break was barely discernible but, in the centre of it was a break he recognized. A pickaxe *had* been swung at the rock. That was how the chunk had been gouged out the first time. Refitted, it stayed snugly in position. Neither a high wind nor driving rain could unsettle it. He had, and only because he had leaned against it.

As somebody once said, he reflected, the unexpected sometimes happens.

How rich was this find? He had no way of guessing. Only a trained geologist with experience in such matters could determine its potential value. This cluster of rock could yield a couple of thousand dollars' worth of ore – or a fortune.

The Kenricks knew nothing of it; of that he was certain. And why assume Buck Brister or any of his men were aware there was gold to be found here? A third party, yes, that seemed far more likely, and could explain a lot. Motive, for instance, for turning neighbour against neighbour, fanning the fires of hostility to fever-heat. If Phil Brister died on a gallows for the Siddons murder, there'd be no holding his father. Open war would be declared with Brister the eventual victor and the Kenricks wiped out, their home and crops burned. In that reduced condition, an offer to buy Kenrick's ravaged acres might be welcomed. But the new owner would not be planting crops nor grazing cattle. Only one section of Kenrick land was of concern to him.

While finishing his cigarette, he prowled around the whole cluster, intently studying surfaces of rocks. He found not one bullet scar, that unmistakeable scar scored by a bullet when it glances off a hard surface, ricocheting. This too was significant, he decided. If Circle B nighthawks had fired on Kenrick guards after dark, they'd never have risked causing such tell-tale scarring if they knew the secret of the rocks, which they probably didn't. And the real snipers would be even more careful, doing their shooting farther west of the cluster.

Remounting, he started for the county seat at an easy pace and mentally reviewed his theories. That was the hell of it. Theories. Nothing he could prove. Well, he could certainly prove those rock clumps were probably worth mining. But that was all.

Prowse and his crew? He disciplined himself to think as a detective with some knowledge of the law. Suspicion wasn't enough. Had he confided his suspicions to Red Ed Whitton – not that he had any intention of doing so – that would be Whitton's reaction. Suspicion by itself was worthless. Proof was what mattered.

His decision was reached before he sighted the town. For the time being, it would have to be his and Hattie's secret. Stay patient, play the waiting game until he could devise some means of setting a trap, forcing guilty parties to tip their hand. And that would take a lot of figuring.

It was after 10 a.m. when he returned the chestnut to the livery stable. He did a lot of yawning while walking from there to Hubbard's Hotel and, as he entered the lobby, glanced at the keyrack. Hattie was in her room. Her key would be hanging from its numbered peg were she out and about. He collected his own and made a plea to the desk clerk.

'The dining-room's not open at this time I know, but how're my chances of a sandwich and a cup of coffee in my room?'

'One of the maids'll oblige,' said the clerk. 'Ten minutes, Mister Gavin, maybe sooner.'

Upstairs, he rapped softly at his wife's door. She opened it to eye him expectantly.

'Use the window again,' he muttered. 'A maid'll fetch me coffee and a sandwich presently. When she leaves, we'll talk, but not for long.'

'To hear is to obey, oh, master,' she intoned.

'*You* couldn't compose that comeback.' He grinned tiredly. 'Too trite. It has to be a line out of some old melodrama you played in.'

'Good guess.'

'See you in a little while.'

He let himself into his room, opened the window, unstrapped his weapons and rid himself of hat and jacket. The maid delivered his snack. He had finished it and was removing his boots when Hattie joined him.

'You look bushed,' she observed, lowering the shade. 'So no talk now?'

'Too much to tell you, honey. It's been quite a night and, believe me, the tag-end of it was not exactly dull. Better I hit the feathers. I plan on rousing around mid-afternoon. If you're around at that time, I'll give you a report after I bathe and change.'

'Tell me this much before you and Morpheus get reacquainted. Are we making any progress?'

'Plenty. I've learned a lot, but we can't use it yet. I'll explain later.'

'Sweet dreams, lover.'

'An inspiration'd be the sweetest dream. That's what I'm gonna need – inspiration.'

Hattie left by the window. Rick slept.

Chris Dewkes was doing it again around 2.30 that afternoon, loitering by the schoolyard fence, which proved fortunate for the new schoolteacher.

She had been on his mind since he first laid eyes on her. The junior deputy had been an eager-to-learn student in his own schooldays and, thanks to his preoccupation with books, was better educated than his boss or Deputy Schumack. Some locals, though duly respectful of his badge of office, regarded him as a colourless young man, husky, handy with a gun when needs be, but lacking imagination. They were wrong. Christopher Melville Dewkes had plenty of imagination and a lively intelligence camouflaged by his stolid demeanour.

Analyzing his own feelings, he supposed he was in love. From all he'd read, wasn't this how men in love felt about one special woman? Couldn't get her off his mind. No raving beauty, Miss Min, but that didn't seem to matter. She appealed to him in a way no other woman ever had. He maintained, as befitted all lawmen, a protective attitude to every female citizen of Greco County. Part of his duty.

But, when he thought of Miss Min, that protective feeling was much stronger. Every woman's welfare was important, but hers more than all the others.

Therefore, when his ears caught the sounds erupting from the schoolhouse, the voices of older boys raised in anger, a younger girl screaming, the schoolteacher desperately demanding order, he reacted promptly, didn't make for the gate, just vaulted the fence and ran to the schoolhouse doorway as fast as his legs could carry him.

He charged into a scene of violence. Smaller children had quit their desks and retreated to corners of the schoolroom, obviously intimidated. A little girl was weeping in alarm. Minerva Platt was trying in vain to reassure the young ones and separate two hefty boys wrestling fiercely.

'Stop that!' she commanded, grasping at them. 'Marvin – Thadeus – stop it this instant!'

She was too close for comfort. The brawling boys lurched against her, throwing her off-balance. Before Dewkes could reach her, she had collided with a desk and fallen. She was pallid and trembling when he reached her and helped her to her feet.

'Stand clear now, Miss Min,' he urged. 'Leave 'em to me.'

'They're like – savages!' she gasped.

The combatants couldn't prevail against the deputy's bulk and muscle-power. He broke their holds and separated them, gripping them by their collars and forcing them out of arms' length of each other. Roughly, he shook them. They eyed him apprehensively.

'How'd you like to do your brawling in a cell of the county jail?' he growled. 'Think you're too young to be arrested? Don't count on it. Answer up now, or jail's where you'll be. What're you fighting about?'

At close quarters, his brawn and his grim expression demoralized Marvin and Thadeus; they were tongue-tied. Minerva, now seated and holding the weeping girl on her lap, spoke bitterly.

'I can answer your question, Deputy. In the middle of our English lesson, when they should have been paying attention to me, they began arguing. It seems Marvin admires farm folk and Thadeus regards cattlemen as – in his own words – more important than no-account sodbusters. He called Marvin a jackass and – and they flew at each other and – it was disgraceful!'

'I'm gonna say this just once,' Dewkes threatened the boys. 'You young bigmouths act up like this ever again, it's the jailhouse for you, and Sheriff Whitton'll have plenty to say to your fathers. Now you – all of you kids – settle down, get back to your lessons and heed everything Miss Min's trying to teach you.'

He released the scrappers. Subdued now, they returned to their desks, as did the other children. He doffed his Stetson to the teacher and, after she followed him to the doorway, addressed her gently, enquiring if she had suffered injury. She replied quietly, but vehemently.

'Physically – a few bruises I've no doubt. But bruises fade, Deputy …'

'Dewkes, Miss Min. First name's Christopher. I'm called Chris.'

'… but a shock to the nerves does not heal quickly. I'm outraged by the behaviour of those boys. And disgusted – to think a disagreement between a rancher and a farmer could have such an effect on mere schoolboys.'

'Well now, you just calm yourself, Miss Min, and don't be frightened. When school's out, you'll find me right by this door. I'd call it a privilege to walk you to your boarding-house.'

'If you escort me, Deputy Dewkes, it will be straight to Mayor Ventry's office.'

'Wherever you want to go, I'll be here.'

From then until Minerva set her pupils free and locked up, Dewkes was a worried man. As was his way, he kept his apprehensions to himself and, when the teacher came out, wearing her bonnet and shawl, fumbling with the key as she locked the door, tried to offer comfort.

'An isolated incident, Miss Min. Please don't assume there'll be a repetition.'

'You have a good command of English which does you credit,' she murmured. 'Thank you for your efforts to reassure me, but I am *not* reassured. That ugly scene was – just too much. I can't endure any more.'

They had left the schoolyard and were approaching Main Street before he dared ask, 'Do you *have* to talk to the mayor?'

'I beg your pardon, Deputy Dewkes?' she frowned.

'Sorry,' he apologized. 'Speaking out of turn. Not for me to ask.'

'What choice do I have?' she challenged. 'How can I hope to teach children under these conditions? I can't control those bigger boys. They outweigh me. It's become a hopeless situation. I just can't carry on.'

'You wouldn't think of...?'

'A male teacher is the only answer. It's all too much for me. I've no option but to tender my resignation and seek a post elsewhere.'

'No, don't do that.'

He spoke impulsively, couldn't hold it back. They were entering Main Street now, she eyeing him sidelong, her brows raised.

'Really, Deputy Dewkes.'

'My apologies again, Miss Min,' he muttered. 'You'll be thinking I'm taking liberties. It's just – maybe it's too soon for you to give up.'

'This terrible feud....'

'It can't last forever. And this is fine country and Greco's a good town for a lady like you. In your shoes, I'd ...'

'You're about to advise me – on such short acquaintance?'

'It's just a notion, Miss Min.'

'Oh, very well. Whatever it is, I'll give you an A for good intentions.'

'You have a right to complain to Mayor Ventry. But, instead of resigning, you could just threaten to. Make it an ultimatum. He does something about the feud, or else. He'd have to heed you. You've got an edge on him.'

'An edge?'

'An advantage. Wouldn't be easy for him to find somebody to take your place. You're needed here.'

Minerva thought about that till they reached City Hall. As they entered the building, Seth Arundell was descending the stairs. Dewkes performed introductions; the storekeeper-councilman had not yet met the new schoolteacher. Arundell greeted Minerva politely and, in response to the deputy's question, replied, 'Sure. I've just been talking to

Josiah. He's upstairs in his office.'

She spoke again as they climbed the stairs.

'I'll do as you suggested. It may not change anything, but I'll try.'

'Worth the effort,' he said earnestly. 'And you're entitled to make your feelings known.'

Moments later, he was knocking on the door of Mayor Ventry's private office and being invited to enter. He ushered Minerva in and, at once, Ventry was the typical urbane and hospitable civic leader, rising from behind his desk, showing his visitors an affable smile, gesturing them to chairs.

'A pleasure, Miss Platt. Nice of you to pay me a call. Happy in your work, I take it?'

Dewkes held a chair for her, seated himself and set his Stetson on his knees, while Minerva fixed indignant eyes on the mayor and declared she was seriously considering resigning and leaving Greco to seek a more orderly community.

'My dear lady ...' he began.

But she was not to be distracted. Grimly, she recounted all details of the commotion during class, the cause of it and her efforts to deter the fist-swinging belligerents. And ended her statement by complaining that, after being knocked to the floor, she would most certainly have been trampled upon but for the timely intervention of Deputy Dewkes.

'It will not do, Mayor Ventry. It is worse than unseemly. Such behaviour in a schoolroom is barbaric, terrifying for the younger children and – and completely intolerable!'

'I'm most desperately sorry,' frowned Ventry who, till now, had thought her to be timid and reticent. 'Mighty unfortunate experience for you,

Miss Platt, but those younger children need you. I'll help every way I can if you'll please forget it and – uh – reconsider your decision to quit.'

Dewkes coughed apologetically and threw in his ten cents' worth. It was the first time in Ventry's memory that the quiet lawman had addressed him so bluntly.

'It's pretty much up to you, sir. Shouldn't you do some hard talking to Buck Brister and Mace Kenrick?'

'Up to me?' challenged Ventry. 'Up to the sheriff – and his assistants. Well, I agree it's a crisis of great concern to the administration, but maybe you're forgetting I've already made a personal appeal to the warring parties.'

'I believe Sheriff Whitton'll brace 'em again,' said Dewkes. 'But isn't it time for you to try again, come down heavier on them?'

'All this rivalry is – like a contagious disease, don't you see?' Minerva said bitterly. 'And the disease is spreading. It could affect the whole community and it's already affecting the young ones. Those two boys, Marvin and Thadeus, seemed to be friends before this happened. Now they've turned on each other, come to blows during class, brawling like drunken men in a saloon.'

'Most regrettable,' nodded Ventry. 'That'll be Marvin Ingram the lawyer's son and Thadeus Arundell, the storekeeper's youngest son. I'll speak to the parents, Miss Platt, you have my word. And, yes, I'll certainly visit Circle B and the Kenrick farm again. I'll do my utmost, dear lady, if only you'll reconsider ...'

'Two weeks,' said Minerva, her eyes gleaming.

'Pardon?' blinked Ventry.

'Two weeks,' she repeated, rising. 'If, by that time, the trouble at Greco Canyon has not been settled, you'll have my written resignation to present to the school board.'

'Are you sure you...?' he began.

'Mayor Ventry, teaching is my profession and some people have been kind enough to say I'm dedicated,' she declared. 'I love children and it's always my dearest wish that they'll make something of themselves and become responsible adults. That can only be achieved by education and I want to do my part. But, dedicated as I am, I'm also frightened. The atmosphere created by the rancher, the farmer and those who support them is so – so ominous. This is a very real crisis and, until it's resolved, law-abiding people are at risk. I'm getting the impression the tension has become too familiar to the citizens. They're getting used to it, perhaps accepting it, becoming apathetic about it.'

'For pity's sake.' The mayor was taken aback. 'That's a mighty harsh thing to say.' But he raised a hand placatingly. 'Please. I'm not dismissing your opinion. Maybe Greco folk're becoming a tad too fatalistic for their own good.'

'Give it some thought,' she advised. Dewkes was out of his chair and opening the door for her. 'And please remember I mean what I say. Two more weeks is as much as I can endure. Good afternoon to you, Mayor Ventry.'

She was trembling as they descended the stairs. Dewkes knew it; his right hand was cupped under her left elbow.

'Just – uh – take it easy,' he pleaded. 'Things'll get better.'

'I'm right, you know,' she sighed. 'People of the

big cities along the east and west coasts call it the wild west, and that certainly applied to this part of the frontier. The Indian wars seemed to be over. We talk of civilization and progress, but can you call this community civilized?'

'There'll be a big improvement,' he promised. 'Greco'll be the kind of town it used to be and you'll learn to like it.'

From City Hall, he escorted her to the side street on which was located the Chester boarding-house. And now, finally, it occurred to her, 'If I may say so, Deputy Dewkes, you seem to be somewhat personally concerned about my ultimatum to the mayor.'

'Well, Miss Min, being an officer of the law....'

'I said *personally* concerned.'

'All right, yes, that's true enough.'

They turned into the side street, he moving slowly to enable her to keep pace with him.

'May I ask why?' she demanded.

An awkward moment for him; he was regretting never having developed a smooth approach, a relaxed and reassuring way with the opposite sex. However he expressed himself, it would probably sound clumsy, or too blunt.

'I just don't want you to leave Greco,' he muttered.

'I understand you're a bachelor. You have no children attending the county school, so what difference would it make to you?'

'I just don't want you to go, Miss Min.'

'You aren't answering my question.'

'Well....'

'Yes?'

'The thing is – I'd miss you.'

She came to a halt at the front gate of the boarding-house, no longer trembling, but definitely startled.

'Good heavens,' was all she could say.

'Meaning no offence,' he hastened to assure her. 'Give you my word, Miss Min, I never spoke this way to a lady before.'

'You'd – miss me?' she asked uneasily.

'Wouldn't say it if I didn't mean it,' he declared.

'Deputy Dewkes....'

'I'm called Chris mostly.'

'Excuse me. I have an aversion, perhaps a foolish aversion, to shortened names. I don't mind my pupils addressing me as Miss Min but, if you wish me to use your given name, I'd prefer you called me Minerva.'

'I'd be honoured,' he said humbly.

'Christopher, I'm plain of face and unaccustomed to....' Despite her extensive vocabulary, she had to pause to choose the right word. 'To overtures of this kind. And the last time a man showed such interest in me, it was a distressing experience.'

'He was too forward,' he guessed.

'I was unaware, at least at the start, he had a wife and children,' she confided.

He nodded understandingly.

'A lady like you would never take kindly to that.'

'And you should try to be practical,' she warned. 'I did not exaggerate when I told Mayor Ventry of my feelings, how frightened I am. The ultimatum – well – that was the frightened woman talking. People tell me those canyon men have hated each other for two years. I'm not such an optimist as to believe the trouble could be laid to rest in two weeks. So then – I'm sorry – but I *will* be leaving, which means ...'

'But....'

'... which means – I think you do realize what it means, Christopher. There'd be no point in our becoming close friends.'

'Two weeks.' He opened the gate for her and doffed his Stetson. 'There might be something done between now and then. Maybe *I* haven't done as much as I should.'

'No.' She shook her head sadly. 'I'm sure you, the sheriff and the other deputy have done as much as can be expected of you. It's just so hopeless.'

Dewkes watched her move up the flagged path to the porch and into the house, then turned to walk back to Main Street. Something, he kept repeating to himself. He had to do something. She was the kind of woman who, having made a decision, would hold to it. Two weeks from now, she would leave Greco. He would never see her again, would lose all chance of courting her. Unless....

As he hurried to the *Times* office, he paid no attention to the vehicle moving westward along Main. Mayor Ventry's buggy; he was headed for the canyon.

Editor Upshaw was bemused when confronted by the junior deputy. Half-way through Dewkes's plea, he cut him short.

'You don't have to persuade me. The mayor already did. He was in here a few minutes ago demanding that the *Times* should make a forceful plea to Brister and Kenrick in the next edition. I'm to remind them – again – of what their feud's doing to the Greco community.'

'Make it strong,' urged Dewkes. 'You know what I mean. Big headline. "Greco County In Jeopardy". Something like that.'

'Hey, chief, that's a helluva notion for a headline,' remarked the typesetter.

'We'll use it,' Upshaw decided. 'Satisfied, Chris?'

'It can only help,' said Dewkes.

By suppertime, refreshed by sleep, a cool bath, a shave and a change of clothing, Rick had an appetite and a great deal to tell his wife.

6

The Ideal Ally

It wasn't the same corner table in the hotel dining-room but, provided they spoke quietly, there was no danger other diners would overhear.

Hattie managed to absorb it all without threat to her digestion, every aspect of everything Rick told her of his scouting expedition, its aftermath and his hunches. He overlooked nothing. They were husband and wife, but also detectives in partnership; he neither exaggerated nor understated.

Only when he had said it all did she make the predictable comment.

'It's progress, a lot of progress, but there's much you can't be certain of. Bar 9 shapes up as prime suspect, but Judy's daddy or any other law officer would say your hunches aren't worth a hill of beans without proof positive. And any lawyer would dismiss the evidence you've dug up as circumstantial.'

'I'm resigned to that, sweetheart.'

'And you daren't – *we* daren't – breathe a word to anybody about your big discovery.'

'The situation's touchy enough already. If word

got out, it could only worsen. The Kenricks would be battling hundreds of trespassers. That kind of news is apt to start a – you know what I mean.'

'Gold rush.' Hattie leaned close and whispered it. 'The sanest citizens would catch the fever. Townsmen and ranch-hands would go haywire and Red Ed's problems would multiply, not just day by day, but hour by hour.'

'Tough as he is, he *could* suffer a seizure,' opined Rick. 'That'd displease me, honey. He doesn't like me, but I admire him. And I'd be just as sorry for us. The Braddock Detective Agency would be saying "*Adios, mucho dinero*". No fat bonus from our client.'

'You said our best course would be to set up a trap, bulldog the guilty parties into tipping their hand,' she reminded him. 'Any ideas?'

'It's still our best bet,' he insisted. 'But no, Hattie. No ideas yet. I need time to figure all the angles, come up with a strategy. Meanwhile, we've no option but to keep what we know a secret.'

'So,' shrugged Hattie. 'It's too early for me to compose another reassuring letter to our clients.'

On duty at the Oriental that night, they performed their roles of house dealer and entertainer to Jarrow's satisfaction; when their Greco assignment was brought to a happy conclusion, when they collected what pay was due them, they could claim they had earned every dime of it, given value for money.

Rick took his turn at several games, supervising the dice layout from seven till nine, working the roulette table for an hour, then working the rest of his shift as house dealer in a poker party.

Hattie was, as usual, at her best, in good voice,

her popularity soaring. Waldo Gooch's accompaniment was as expert as ever, though he was watery-eyed and, more than once, played only the base notes on his piano, fishing out a handkerchief with his other hand and coughing into it.

Mid-morning of the morrow, the next edition of the *Times* began circulating and, to the gratification of Deputy Dewkes, Roger Upshaw had used the banner headline he suggested. GRECO COUNTY IN JEOPARDY was emblazoned above the editor's dramatic analysis of the current crisis, which Dewkes, his boss, Deputy Schumack and the whole population read with keen interest.

Dewkes gave Upshaw due credit for composing an attention-winning story. But one detail irked him. Obviously, Mayor Ventry had informed Upshaw of Minerva's ultimatum, with the predictable result. Upshaw had decided the ruffianly conduct of two pupils, the treatment she had suffered, plus the ultimatum, rated a two-column report on page two. Dewkes feared Minerva would be dismayed by this publicity. He didn't want her dismayed, didn't want her bothered in any way. About anything.

He was in his boss's office when Mayor Ventry stopped by to talk of his visits to the rival factions yesterday afternoon.

'Did it all again, Ed, and said it all again,' he muttered, slumped in the chair in front of the sheriff's desk. 'Tried reasoning, tried warning them of the possible dire consequences of their continuing hostility, even threw in a threat or two.'

'Like talkin' to a coupla brick walls,' guessed Whitton. 'And wouldn't *I* know? I've tried as hard as you, Josiah.'

'I'm beginning to believe there's nothing more we can do,' fretted Ventry. 'Can you think of anything else…?'

'The hell with 'em all.' Whitton didn't look worried, just pugnacious. 'They'd better keep their damn-blasted quarrel cooped in the canyon. If they keep bringin' their mean tempers to town, startin' fights in bar-rooms, stables, stores or on Main Street, we'll give 'em misery and plenty of it.'

'Make 'em whine,' growled Gil Keece, entering from the cellblock at that moment. 'You and Nate and Chris're tough enough to round up as many of 'em as disturb the peace.'

'When we lock 'em up, it won't be till just next mornin',' Whitton assured the mayor. 'We'll do what we've done before, charge 'em and hold 'em for the circuit judge. Mightn't help much, then again it might. Only holdin' one prisoner right now, so …'

'We got plenty room for more,' leered Keece.

'With a lot of their hired hands in jail – and it takes plenty of 'em to work Brister's range and Kenrick's land, them fools'll maybe stop and think. Seems to me they ain't done much smart thinkin' since they first locked horns.'

'I was hoping things wouldn't get any worse,' said Ventry. 'Then came the murder of that Kenrick hand.' He glanced to the jailhouse entrance. 'Young Brister still protesting his innocence?'

'He ain't about to oblige us with a confession, that's for damn sure,' said Whitton. 'Horrie Ingram's in there with him now. Fine by me. County attorney says give 'em plenty time together, work out as good a defence as they can. It's gonna be a fair trial, Josiah.'

'Whatever the jury's verdict, the peace of Greco County will still be at risk,' complained Ventry. 'If he's found guilty, Brister will never forgive Kenrick. If he's acquitted, Kenrick will never forgive Brister. The feud will continue – indefinitely.' He got to his feet. 'The administration must maintain a cordial relationship with the press. I'd best look in on Upshaw and congratulate him on this latest appeal to the antagonists.'

When the mayor departed, Whitton nodded to Keece. 'Shut that door, Gil. Ingram and the kid're entitled to privacy.'

The sheriff and his staff could justly claim to have extended full co-operation to the prisoner's defence counsel. A table and chair had been installed in Phil Brister's cell. Lawyer Horace Ingram, a well-groomed individual, double-chinned and more than a little overweight, was free to consult with his client as often and for as long as he wished. And was doing so. Ingram, though a family man, was dedicated to his profession. When a case came his way, he gave it everything; it was fortunate that his wife was a woman of great patience, making allowance for his long periods of preoccupation.

Phil Brister sat on his bunk, answering his lawyer's questions, watching him take notes. One year older than the girl he loved, he was lean and shorter than his brothers. The face under the tousled hair was even-featured, sensitive.

'You keep saying it, Mister Ingram,' he muttered. 'It'll be a tough case. I know it, so you don't have to tell me.'

'Tough, boy, but I'm no quitter.' Ingram pocketed his pencil. 'There are a few holes I can make in the county's evidence against you, and you can be damn sure I will. Something that could work for us, could make a big impression on the jury – if you're willing – would be for you to take the stand and the oath and testify in your own defence. How do you feel about that?'

'Wouldn't bother me one little bit,' declared Phil. 'Why should I fear telling the truth?'

'You'll be at ease with me,' said Ingram. 'You're used to me. You know I'm on your side. But Mister Prosecutor'll have the right to cross-examine. I don't know if you've attended any trials here....' Phil shook his head. 'So you've never seen the county attorney in action, nor heard him fire questions at a witness, confuse him, put the fear of hell into him. Are you ready for that?'

'I think I can handle it.'

'Mat O' Sullivan's shrewd and tricky, an expert at belittling a witness, needling him, destroying his confidence.'

'Yes, sir, I understand. You tell me what I should do, I'll do it.'

'What you shouldn't do, what you daren't do, is lose your temper. You're a thoughtful young feller, Phil. Right from the start, you've kept your nerve. But you've never been tongue-lashed by a spellbinder like Mat.'

'Something I already figured out for myself, Mister Ingram. Playing tough in court'd look bad for me. I plan on being polite to everybody, including Mister O' Sullivan.'

'Smart boy. Don't let yourself be intimidated. He puts on quite a show and I can only assume Judge Drake enjoys it, because he gives Mat too much leeway for my liking. Mat'll wave his arms, roll his eyes, rant and rage and, at regular intervals, give you the accusing finger routine.' Ingram demonstrated by thrusting out an arm with a forefinger aimed at Phil's face. 'Just part of his scare tactics. Don't let it throw you.'

'I'll remember,' promised Phil.

'He'll claim the evidence against you is damning,' predicted Ingram. 'I'll keep reminding the court it's circumstantial and a hell of a long way from conclusive.'

'Because you believe my statement,' Phil said gratefully.

'Well, young feller,' shrugged the lawyer. 'I go by my instincts. You heard the shot, saw the gunflash, fired at the shooter and took off after him, and then Jethro Kenrick headed you off. I can imagine that. What I can't imagine is you lining your rifle on Siddons and backshooting him. For me, it doesn't ring true.'

'You'll be saying that?' asked Phil.

'In my opening address to the jury,' nodded Ingram. 'It could make an impression. You can bet I'll do my damnedest. And there's another point that could swing the decision your way. You hated the whole thing, you told me, your kin turning against the Kenricks, and vice versa.'

'A feud.' Phil grimaced uneasily. 'Bad medicine, Mister Ingram. Good people get hurt. In the end, nobody wins.'

Ingram lit a cigar and eyed him curiously.

'This is personal, just between us, so you don't have to answer it. A big question. How in blazes could you and Martha Kenrick keep your relationship a tight secret? It couldn't have been easy.'

'It was *never* easy,' winced Phil. 'We knew each other from back when we were at school. Sundays, before church, we'd talk some. That was up till a couple of years ago when the feud started. After that, with both of us fretting about the whole thing, we got closer, but our fathers got mad if we tried to talk to each other.'

'So, from then on, you had to meet in secret.'

'We'd trade notes any time we got the chance. I'd let her know if I'd be fishing at Little Rock Bend Sunday afternoons. If she could get away, she'd come along. There were other places like the line shack Circle B doesn't use any more. It's on a lonesome part of our west quarter. When she could manage it, we'd meet there. We didn't do anything wrong....'

'I believe you.'

'But we talked a lot, talked of how we wished our fathers'd stop hating each other, so we could get married.'

'You know, Phil, that could go right to their hearts. The jurymen I mean. Some of them will be family men who'll be reminded of their own courting days. Good angle. The sentimental touch.'

'No, sir,' Phil said firmly. 'I don't want Martha called to testify and being gawked at – not unless some mean-minded witness hints we were doing anything we oughtn't have.'

'Whatever you say,' soothed Ingram. 'But, while we're on the subject, Phil, *I* can be sentimental sometimes. Just want you to know this. If I get you acquitted, if this feud can be settled so that you youngsters can set a wedding date, I'd appreciate an invitation.'

'You can depend on it,' said Phil.

Rising to leave, the lawyer told him they'd be talking again next day. He had been advised by Ed Whitton that the circuit judge was expected in approximately three weeks, so the defence had ample time for preparing its case.

At the Oriental that evening, the Braddocks were faced with a temporary dilemma. The off-duty Deputy Dewkes, preoccupied though he was with thoughts of Minerva Platt, became an interested observer. Also on hand was the irascible Ansell Frickett, MD.

Rick was supervising at the roulette layout, Hattie halfway through her third song, when Waldo Gooch sneezed, coughed wheezily and gave up on trying to keep up with her. All eyes were on him when she asked solicitously, 'You all right, Waldo?'

'Keep playin' for her, Waldo!' ordered a ranch-hand. 'We rode in to hear her sing!'

'Everybody stay patient,' begged Jarrow, approaching the piano. 'Waldo, you don't look so good.'

'And I feel like I look,' panted the piano player; he had to wait for his coughing to subside to get those words out.

'I think Waldo's caught a chill,' frowned Hattie.

Jarrow called to Frickett, who was beelining for a vacated chair at a poker table.

'Hey, Doc, come take a look at him.'

'Connie's probably right – just a chill,' said the medico. 'And I'm feeling lucky. This is my night for winning, Jarrow. I'm gonna break your bank, damned if I'm not. By midnight, you'll be ...'

'Don't say poorer,' chided Jarrow. 'Why fool

yourself, Doc? You're the worst poker player in the county and always a loser.'

'That's an insult,' scowled Frickett.

'Not that I object to your big contribution to our profits,' jibed Jarrow.

'Another insult,' complained Frickett.

'But I'll thank you to abide by the ethics of your profession,' said Jarrow. 'We have a sick man here, and you're a doctor.'

'If I can be of assistance ...' began Lippert the undertaker.

'Thanks a heap!' gasped Waldo.

'Felix, don't be greedy,' retorted Jarrow. 'Come on, Doc, do your duty.'

Grudgingly, Frickett came to the piano, checked Waldo's pulse and ordered him to open his mouth wide. Waldo obeyed. Frickett's irritation increased.

'Damn,' he scowled.

'How bad?' demanded Jarrow.

'Severe chill,' grouched Frickett. 'Throat raw, nasal passage inflamed. He belongs in bed.' Impatiently, he helped Waldo to his feet. 'Feel up to walking to – I can never remember – which boarding-house?'

'McKillop's on Sabado Street,' sighed Waldo. 'I can make it. Connie honey, I'm sorry I ...'

'Forget it,' soothed Jarrow. 'Connie understands. You go along now and do whatever Doc tells you.'

He helped the musician rise and don his coat while the not so callous of his customers aimed sympathetic glances. Frickett announced he would stop by his surgery for his bag, adding, 'I'll require a small bottle of rum.'

'On the house,' said Jarrow, nodding to the bartender. 'And Doc, whatever it takes to fix what's ailing Waldo, bill me for it.'

Doctor and patient departed. Hattie made to seat herself at the piano, announcing she would accompany herself. Her admirers raised protests. They preferred her being mobile while entertaining, moving around; plainly they were here to look as well as listen. Rick took that as his cue and offered his services.

'I've often played for her, Clint. So, if you'll take over from me....'

'So, along with everything else you can do, you're a musician?' challenged Jarrow. 'Tell me, Sam, is there anything you *can't* do?'

'Certainly,' grinned Rick. 'I can't work a roulette table and play piano at the same time. What do you say?'

'Do it,' urged Jarrow. 'The paying customers're getting restless.'

He took over at the roulette table. Rick perched on the piano stool and traded smiles with his wife.

'What'll it be, Connie? How about "They're Waiting For Me Everywhere"? Maybe these music-lovers never heard it before.'

'Hit it, Professor,' she ordered.

He provided a jaunty introduction and she was back on the job, strutting among her admirers and delivering the lyrics with gusto.

'They're waiting for me everywhere,
And if you're wondering who,
Four and twenty bachelors and a married man
or two ...'

That song and all the others performed to Rick's accompaniment were crowd-pleasers. They made performance number fourteen a duet, he adding his baritone to her contralto in an upbeat rendition of 'Beware Of Laredo Lulu' and, when that one ended, were rewarded with a noisy ovation.

During all this, Dewkes nursed a tankard of beer at the bar with his wistful gaze on the performers, envying them. To a young man so reticent, they seemed to have it all, confidence to spare, high spirits, humour, style. And, obviously, an affectionate relationship. He thought of his deep feelings for the schoolteacher and his fear that she would hold to her decision, pack her bags and quit unless the trouble at Greco Canyon were settled in two weeks.

When, some seventy minutes later, Hattie pleaded she needed to rest, the burly deputy watched her sitting with eight of her goggle-eyed admirers, six townsmen and a couple of cowhands. They eagerly questioned her about her background and all she'd done before coming to Greco and were entertained by her answers, all ad-libbed and as far from the truth as the distance separating New York from San Francisco.

Dewkes drifted across to the piano. Rick still sat there, quietly amusing himself by improvising a slowed-down version of a Mozart melody stuck in his mind. He continued his strumming while Dewkes leaned on the piano and dolefully remarked, 'You don't know how lucky you are, Mr Gavin.'

'Deputy Dewkes isn't it?' asked Rick. 'First name Chris? Call me Sam and, if you have something to be sad about, let it all out. I'm a sympathetic listener.'

'I'm rarely jealous of other people, Sam. But, if I gave into it, I could be mighty jealous of you.'

'Why so?'

'You're a good-looking gent with a lot of class. I'm just a deputy sheriff and lonesome. You and Miss Connie get along fine together. That's what I'm trying to do with – uh – a lady I....'

'A lady you've taken a shine to? If you name her, it'll be our secret, Chris. I'm no blabbermouth.'

'Miss Min, the schoolteacher.'

'I know her. Connie too. We travelled here on the same coach. You have good taste, Chris. She's a nice person.'

'Yeah, but scared stiff. She had to show up here when – you know – things could be a lot more peaceful. Just between us, Sam, I'm so mad at Buck Brister and the farmer, I could ride out there and bust their jaws – and take on any of their sons just for the hell of it. That's what's scaring Miss Min, that damn feud.'

The deputy unfolded his tale of woe, never guessing Rick was more than casually interested, intrigued in fact, and with the germ of an idea stirring in his brain. So the schoolma'am had delivered an ultimatum and, when it came to the courting game, Dewkes was the slow and diffident type, hardly likely to attempt sweeping the lady off her feet inside two weeks. He listened till Dewkes was through airing his grievance before enquiring, 'What kind of a boss is the sheriff? Does he encourage his deputies to show a little initiative, act independently at times, or does he insist you and Schumack do nothing he doesn't tell you to do?'

'That's a peculiar kind of question,' frowned Dewkes.

'What's the answer?' prodded Rick.

'There're plenty of times when we have to act

fast, get something done our own way, make up our own minds about it,' said Dewkes. 'Ed Whitton understands that. He expects us to decide certain things for ourselves.'

'All right,' said Rick. 'I've assured you I can keep a secret. How about you?'

'It'd depend on the secret,' was the deputy's cautious reply.

'Well, for instance,' shrugged Rick. 'I'm starting to get an idea or two about the feud and how to bring it to an end. It could be done, Chris. One small problem though. Red Ed's leery of me, calls me an amateur. So I can't try my strategy on him. I think this plan'll work, but I'll need a sidekick and, given a choice, I'd as soon that sidekick was a lawman. I never work outside the law.'

Dewkes appeared dubious.

'Say nothing to the boss? I don't know, Sam.'

'You don't have to decide here and now. Come visit me after this place closes down. We'll talk it over. If you insist you should consult the sheriff first, no hard feelings on my part. But – till you decide – it's just between us, OK?'

'Well....'

'My room at the Hubbard Hotel. It's a second floor rear. You'll see my light from the back alley. I'll be watching for you anyway.'

'I guess it can't do any harm for me to listen.'

'No harm at all. And, if my plan works, Brister and Kenrick'll be friendly neighbours again and you'll have time aplenty for wooing Miss Min.'

'All right,' nodded Dewkes. 'I'll be there.'

He finished his beer and quit the Oriental, which did thriving business this night until, after midnight, Hattie good-humouredly warned the crowd she would soon be hoarse, unable to sing to them, if she overworked her vocal chords. The last drinker went his way around 12.45 a.m., after which Jarrow and his staff prepared to call it a day, the percentage girls wearily climbing the stairs to their room, the barkeeps stacking chairs atop tables, the housemen donning their hats.

During the time it took them to walk to the hotel, Rick outlined his plan to Hattie. Rarely, if ever, did she question his judgement, but she felt entitled to comment, 'It could be dangerous, Rick.'

'Not with the right back-up,' he insisted. 'I'll miss not having you with me, you know that. To make it work, I need a lawman. And Dewkes is perfect. Carries a badge, sure, but now it's getting personal to him. You could say he has a vested interest in the resolution of the dispute.'

'Whose name is Minerva Platt,' guessed Hattie.

'Show me a man in love, I'll show you a man with incentive,' he grinned.

Before retiring to her own room, she sat with her husband awhile, a deeply concerned Hattie, but outwardly calm while listening to his strategy. When he had finished, she rose and summoned up an encouraging smile. 'Audacious, fiendishly cunning, a typical Rick Braddock set-up. It can't miss.'

'Braddock's rule,' he said cheerfully. 'When you have a suspect, but no proof, force the suspect's hand.'

'My lonely bed awaits,' she said. 'Make your pitch to Deputy Dewkes and, at breakfast, you can tell me if he bought it.'

'He'll buy it,' he predicted.

'Confidence, it's wonderful,' she chuckled.

Left alone, Rick shrugged out of his coat, perched on his window ledge and waited, but not for long. Less than ten minutes later, he heard the deputy's heavy tread on the firestairs. Dewkes appeared on the gallery. They traded nods and, while Rick retreated to squat on the near edge of his bed, Dewkes climbed in, closed the window and helped himself to a chair.

'We won't be overheard,' Rick assured him. 'Draw that chair closer so we can discuss the project quietly.'

Dewkes obeyed, nudged his Stetson off his brow and sat hunched, eyeing Rick solemnly, hanging on his every word. Rick led off by swearing him to secrecy and then confiding his big news, his discovery of pay-ore on Kenrick land. While the deputy's jaw sagged, he emphasized his deep conviction that the Kenricks, the Bristers also, knew nothing of it.

'But there's a third party, Chris. Has to be. And that third party, not Brister nor Kenrick, started the night attacks that triggered the feud for his own reason. We now know what that reason is. In a final flare-up, a bloody showdown, Kenrick would be wiped out. And more receptive to an offer from the third party.'

'Hell's bells,' breathed Dewkes. 'You've withheld information on a crime, what the sheriff'd call the attempted murder of Orin Kenrick, as well as finding gold out there. If Ed Whitton found out....'

'He could do nothing about the shooting,' Rick pointed out. 'No evidence he can act upon, no proof of the sniper's identity. As for the gold, if that news broke, it'd only add to his troubles. He'd have a feud *and* a gold rush to cope with. He's hamstrung. But there's plenty *we* can do, and you wouldn't be breaking any of your boss's rules. You'd be functioning as a law officer.'

'By doing what?' demanded Dewkes.

'I know how to force Prowse's hand.'

'You think Bar 9's behind it all?'

'I did track the sniper to Bar 9.'

'But you said it yourself, Sam, that doesn't prove he's a Bar 9 man. He could've ridden clear of Bar 9 range and farther into the canyon.'

'That's what I said. And, if I'm wrong about Prowse and his crew, we'll come up with nothing. But, if I'm right, the law will have all the evidence Whitton could hope for.'

'And just how do you plan on setting this trap?'

'By making them believe somebody else has stumbled on their big secret. That'll light a fire under them. They'll have no option but to silence Mister Somebody Else. Listen carefully now, Chris.'

Slowly, deliberately, Rick dealt out the details. While trailing the sniper, he had passed a copse on Bar 9 range. If, within those trees, there was a clearing, it would be the ideal site for putting his theory to the test. He talked on until Dewkes could no longer keep his curiosity in check.

'What old prospector're you talking about? There are no prospectors hereabouts.'

'There'll be one,' said Rick. 'He'll call himself Bud Niblo – and you're looking at him.'

Dewkes shrugged helplessly.

'Is that supposed to make sense to me?'

'I'm obliged to confide another little secret,' said Rick. 'I used to be an actor. Character parts, Chris. A disguise? Don't worry, I can do it. In fact, you will see me rig the changes. We'll meet in that copse before tomorrow's dawn. I'll have everything I need. But your horse, you'd better hide it where no Bar 9 hand's apt to spot it, then come on to the clearing afoot.'

'And you think they'll fall for it?' challenged Dewkes.

'I'll be well rehearsed.' Rick grinned wryly. 'It'll be like an invitation, the kind they couldn't refuse.'

The deputy was quiet for a long minute, turning it over in his mind, every audacious, outlandish detail of Rick's strategy. He looked for flaws and found them, but discarded them. It would be worth all the risks, he decided. And he had to accept the logic of Rick's argument. The crisis would continue – indefinitely – unless the instigators of all the trouble, including the cold-blooded murder of a Kenrick hand, were forced out into the open.

'Like an invitation you say,' he mused. 'You aren't afraid they'll want to shut your mouth right away?'

'Blow old Bud out his saddle right there at the ranch-house?' Rick shook his head. 'Why should they, when they can get it done quietly? They'll know where to find me.'

'You're quite a strategist, Sam,' muttered Dewkes. 'Beats me why you aren't a Pinkerton instead of a sporting man.'

'Think you can find your way to that copse?' asked Rick.

'That canyon's never been a strange place for me,' said Dewkes. 'I know every mile of it and the location and boundaries of every spread. You don't have to worry about my finding a safe hideaway for my horse or joining you on time.'

'Something I should've asked before,' said Rick. 'You happen to know how big an outfit Prowse controls?'

'The ramrod, Abelson, and seven hired hands,' was the prompt reply. 'If your hunch is right and they're all in on it, we'd be going up against nine. You can forget about old Lew, the chuckboss. Chances are he knows nothing. Even if he did, he'd be no danger. He can rustle up meals, but that's about all. Rheumatics, you know? He'd be no use with a gun.'

'So,' said Rick, eyeing him steadily. 'You're in? Remember my promise, Chris. I'll make Whitton understand that, at all times, you acted as a responsible law officer. And remember Miss Min.'

'I'm not about to forget *her*,' Dewkes assured him. 'So I'm in. I'll be there when you need me. One last question?'

'Go ahead,' offered Rick.

'If everything works out as planned, what of the gold?' prodded Dewkes. 'That mess of rocks is on Kenrick land. He has a right ...'

'He'll be told – by me,' said Rick. 'I'll also be handing him some advice which I'm pretty sure he'll heed. Mace Kenrick's as much a blusterer as Brister, but he's nobody's fool.'

'Heaven help Greco County if Roger Upshaw gets wind of it,' Dewkes declared as he quit his chair. 'He'd have a big story and – in no time at all – this'd be a trouble town.'

'Kenrick'll be first to be told,' vowed Rick. 'Whatever he decides – well – I'll help him decide, and I'm willing to bet he'll fall in with my suggestion.' Dewkes moved across to raise the window. 'I'll be seeing you?'

'Where you said, at the time you said,' nodded Dewkes.

After the deputy went his way, Rick prepared to turn in. And, mentally, he was still preparing himself.

7

Alias Bud Niblo

It pleased Hattie that, over breakfast, Rick's mood was zesty and optimistic. He had already explained his ruse. Now he was able to announce that he had won the support and co-operation of a reliable ally. She was proud of her man. Whatever apprehension she felt was camouflaged by her serene smile.

At the end of the meal, he told her, 'Little shopping expedition this morning.'

'Props,' she surmised.

'Who'd understand better than you?' he suggested. 'It has to be a convincing performance, sweetheart, so everything about good ol' Bud Niblo has to be well and truly in character.'

'Will you resort to the grey wig and...?'

'No reason I shouldn't. Only the Bristers and Kenricks met Deacon Pitch. Different costume of course, and Bud'll be considerably older than the preacher.'

'Practice the croaky voice, lover. And the body movements are important. A prospector past his prime would be creaky, more than a little rheumaticky. But you can do it. You're a fine actor. A little hammy sometimes, but ...'

'Don't sass me, girlie.' Rick dropped his voice and affected the quavery whine of a grumpy old timer. 'Any more o' your lip, consarn you, I'll paddle your butt, and you better believe it.'

She fluttered her eyelashes at him.

'Hey, that could be *interesting*.'

'Don't play the seductress,' he good-humouredly chided, reverting to his normal voice. 'This isn't the time or the place.'

After breakfast, he made his purchases with care. The hardware store he patronized was on a side street; he chose it after reading the faded, hand-printed sign in the window. As well as brand-new tools of all kinds, second-hand gear was also available here, guaranteed still useable and fairly priced.

The hardware merchant was bemused.

'Oldest pickaxe and spade I can find?' he challenged. 'Mister, if you're down on your luck, you don't look it. So why not a brand-new...?'

'I know what I want,' Rick told him. 'Throw in a tatty old piece of canvas about four feet by three, give me your word you won't discuss our little transaction with any other customers, and I'll sweeten the price you quote.'

'If that's how you like to do business, you got a deal,' grinned the storekeeper. 'Let's take a look out back.'

He was intrigued by Rick's selection. The pickaxe and spade wrapped in the tattered canvas he unearthed showed rust.

'About three feet of twine,' ordered Rick. 'And it doesn't have to be new.'

This too was supplied. Rick had him wrap it all in old newspaper, invited him to name his price and paid $5 extra.

'Just for keeping my mouth shut?'

'One of those times, friend. Silence is golden.'

'Well, you're the customer.'

After stashing his purchases in his room, Rick ventured forth again. It took him close to fifteen minutes to find what had to be Greco's lowliest livery stable. The barn was dismal and the Mexican hostler's eyes heavy-lidded; he seemed the type who had made a career of laziness.

Indicating the animal of his choice, a dun whose best days were way back there somewhere, he questioned the stablehand in Spanish. Was this discouraged-looking animal capable of travelling any distance? Not a great distance, he was told. A hundred miles would be too far. Anywhere within the county, the dun could be ridden there and back, if the rider renting him were in no great hurry. Fernando was beyond a fast gallop, could trot some distance – some short distance – and that was it.

Rick selected the oldest saddle for hire and gave the stablehand instructions, also payment in advance plus a tip that would ensure his instructions would be heeded. He, Samuel Gavin, would come for this horse later. He could not be sure just when; any time between midnight and dawn. No necessity for the stablehand to saddle up for him. This was agreeable to the stablehand, who planned on being fast asleep at that time. That time, or at any other time at which he could sneak a catnap.

Back in his room again, Rick packed various

items into a valise, his make-up box, a felt hat so old, so battered and dirty, that he could never discard it. Too handy, too much in character with the role he intended playing. A bandanna almost as old. Levis showing several patches and a wool blouse that had seen better days, a great many of them. To complete the ensemble, a frayed vest of colourless, worsted material, which would effectively conceal his shoulder holster.

Hattie tapped at the door and entered. Scorning preamble, she insisted, 'You'll need more than the one pistol.'

'Taking both along,' he assured her. 'The mining tools'll be partly visible, wrapped in the old canvas slung to the horse's right side. The Colt'll be hidden in there – within easy reach. Don't worry about me, honey.'

'I'm not worrying,' she lied. 'So, when the sun rises, curtain up?'

'That's when I'll change,' he nodded. 'The deputy's in for a rare experience. It'll be the first time he sees a man assume another identity right before his eyes.'

'I like Deputy Dewkes,' she said. 'But I hope he keeps the ready-for-action lawman well separated from Minerva's suitor. He's smitten and preoccupied, Rick.'

'When the chips're down, he'll concentrate on business,' Rick predicted. 'Minerva's my ace in the hole. It's for her sake he's in cahoots with me. Not that Chris is the kind who wants to make a hero of himself, but he has ample incentive. We lift the lid off the whole conspiracy, stop Brister and Kenrick from making war on each other, bring the feud to a decisive conclusion, and Minerva stays – to be respectfully courted by a worthy man. I believe they'll be good for each other, those two.'

'A successful conclusion will be good for Judy Hargrove's nerves,' remarked Hattie. 'Red Ed will be a happier sheriff and his son-in-law will appreciate our efforts. We're getting closer to that fat bonus?'

'This'll do it,' he said confidently. 'It feels right, sweetheart, it's all coming together. All my hunches'll pay off, you'll see.'

'Greco people know us as good friends,' she reminded him. 'So it won't seem unusual if we stroll along to that Mexican restaurant opposite City Hall today. The cuisine here is good enough, but I'm in the mood for chilli con carne. So – we go out for lunch?'

'Sounds fine to me,' he grinned.

'But, after lunch, you should take an afternoon nap again,' she suggested. 'Waldo's still laid up, so you'll be accompanying me again tonight. Unless I fake a sudden attack of laryngitis, we could still be performing at one o'clock, or even later.'

'Wise notion,' he approved.

Around noon, people on Main Street observing the Braddocks arm-in-arm, bound for the Mexican café, assumed them to be a handsome gambler and a lushly beautiful saloon singer without a care in the world. Rick was as relaxed as he appeared to be; not so Hattie, whose serenity was a façade. Had her admittedly astute but always adventurous husband over-estimated his chances this time? She had, at the time of their less than conventional wedding, promised to love, honour and obey. When they set themselves up as a husband and wife detective agency, she had promised she would never distract her man with pleas that he should be cautious at all times, count the risks, take no wild chances – all the traditional admonitions voiced by wives whose husbands embark on perilous enterprises.

She had kept that promise. Right now, however, she had misgivings. Rick's scheme was sure-fire as far as he was concerned but, womanlike, she feared for his safety. The showdown would almost certainly be violent. Shots would be fired. As a gunfighter, Rick was fast, cool-nerved and accurate, but not bullet-proof. Therefore, she was already devising her own back-up strategy.

They enjoyed their lunch at the Café El Paloma, whose proprietor, studying them covertly, waxed sentimental. To his spouse, he remarked, 'He so *hermoso*, she *muy bello*, both so young. They should be more than friends. He should take her for his *esposa*.'

He spoke softly, but Rick's hearing was acute.

'The owner of this place is a romantic,' he informed Hattie. 'Just remarked to his wife that I ought to marry you.'

'At the acting game, maybe we're better than we realize,' she murmured. 'We've come to know a lot of Greco people and none of them suspect we're husband and wife – and all I had to do was take off my wedding ring and put on a black wig.'

'And I just don't look married?' he challenged.

'It's been almost two years,' she replied. 'What if you don't have that married-man look? You could never convince *me* you're a bachelor.'

He rested for most of that afternoon and, after supper, reported for duty with Hattie. This night, he would supervise no gambling layouts.

'Waldo's doing fine, Doc Frickett says,' Jarrow told him. 'Might be back on the job tomorrow night. But, meanwhile, Connie's the extra attraction, so you're her piano man again.'

'You're the boss,' Rick said cheerily, and made for the piano.

There could be no doubting the black-haired beauty with the radiant smile had drawn regular patrons of other saloons to the Oriental. The games of chance did passable business, but the bar was busier, most of the customers preferring to drink and enjoy Hattie's performance.

While accompanying her, Rick surveyed the crowd. He could distinguish between farmhands and cowboys; neither faction was represented tonight. Townsmen aplenty though.

Some forty minutes after midnight, the place began emptying. Men filing out, passing Hattie, paused to trade pleasantries with her. A few aimed friendly nods Rick's way, after which Jarrow and his staff prepared to shut up shop.

Upon their return to the hotel, Hattie lingered in her husband's room, watching him change. He donned his riding clothes and picked up the valise and the canvas-wrapped tools.

'Got everything?' she asked.

'All in the valise,' he assured her. 'Everything I need for the transformation. At first light, Sam Gavin will become Bud Niblo. I hope Chris is ready for that.' He kissed her and held her close for a few moments. 'Get your sleep now, and don't fret yourself about me – nor the action. It's all figured out.'

'When you go into your act, the audience won't applaud,' she warned. 'They'll throw things at you.

Bullets for instance.'

'We'll have an edge, the deputy and me,' he said comfortingly. 'It's called the element of surprise.'

After Hattie retired to her room, he toted his gear downstairs, left his key on the desk and moved out to make his way to the rundown livery stable. The hostler snored in his cubbyhole back of the barn while Rick saddled the dun and secured his valise and the bundle.

Riding for the canyon, he settled for Fernando's pace, slow and plodding. The dun didn't seemed to mind being gone from his stall, sniffed the early morning air, snorted a time or two.

Later, entering the canyon, Rick heard the familiar night sounds again, the rippling of the creek, the occasional lowing of cattle on Circle B range. He chose to let Fernando wade the shallows of the creek, passing the Kenrick acres, steadily advancing to that section of the south bank where, after inflicting a wound on Kenrick's younger son, a rifleman had quit the creek to approach Bar 9.

On Bar 9 range, he made straight for the copse of cottonwood, thankful a cloudbank was obscuring the moon at this time. There was moonlight again when, after guiding his mount through the trees, he found the clearing. Now Fernando could rest, and so could he.

Until the hour before dawn, shrouded in a blanket, he dozed with his back resting against the base of a tree. What brought him awake was the sound of a man creeping through the timber. He maintained his seated posture, his right hand on the butt of his shoulder-holstered Smith & Wesson, until he recognized the muscular man entering the clearing. Greetings were exchanged, but softly.

'All set, Chris?'

'Reckon so. You?'

'I will be, soon as the sun rises. Won't take me long to change my looks. How about your horse?'

'I did as you said. He's too well hidden to be sighted.' Dewkes propped a Winchester against the tree and hunkered close. 'Town's quiet. I'm glad about that. Makes me feel a little less guilty, sneaking out without leaving a note for the sheriff.'

'You've had time for a lot of thinking about everything I told you,' remarked Rick.

'A lot of thinking,' nodded Dewkes.

'Feeling no qualms?'

'None. We'll try this your way, I'll go along with it and – I guess I'm as confident as you.'

Patiently, they waited for the dawn. At first light, Rick snapped the catches and raised the lid of his valise. Then he worked quickly, changing to his aged prospector outfit. The deputy, inspecting the decrepit hat, observed, 'The duds look right, but you'll need more than the old duds.'

The clearing was well lit when Rick produced wig and false whiskers and opened his make-up box.

'I'm no braggart, but this is one of those times I can't help showing off,' he muttered. 'I think you'll be impressed, Chris, but don't overdo it. No applause if you please. We aren't supposed to be here.'

Dewkes followed his deft movements with keen interest. He first worked on his face, greying his brows, adding a few age lines. Next he donned the ash-grey wig. Then, with spirit gum, he attached the flowing moustache and long beard. He took the hat from the bug-eyed Dewkes, donned it, rose to a stoop-shouldered stance and squinted down at him.

'Hol-eee Moses,' breathed Dewkes.

In the nasal, quavery delivery of a man well on in years, Rick asked, 'That who I look like, young feller? Better I look like ol' Bud Niblo, on accounta that's who I am.' Reverting to his natural voice, he enquired, 'How *do* I look? More importantly, how do I sound?'

'You've done it.' Dewkes was deeply impressed. 'With me squatting here watching you, you've done it – changed everything about yourself. Damn it, Sam, you can't be just a gambler!'

'Told you I've done some acting,' said Rick.

'Didn't tell me you were so all-fired expert,' frowned Dewkes.

'If something's worth doing,' shrugged Rick, 'it's worth doing as well as you can manage. We'd better hope Prowse and his crew are just as impressed. They have to believe I'm a burnt-out old fossicker. Who else, poking around this canyon, would think to investigate that rock clump on Kenrick land? And who else but a veteran prospector would identify a pay-vein where that chunk of rock broke away?'

'Well, I share your suspicions about Prowse,' said Dewkes. 'Now you'll prove you're right, won't you? You'll know, Sam. You'll see it in their eyes when you're dropping your bombshell.'

'Delivering my lines,' corrected Rick. 'That's the show business term for it.' He glanced around. 'Sun's well and truly up. If I move in on them now, they could be at breakfast when I show up, or just finishing. Trust me, friend. Some of them are in for a bout of chronic indigestion.'

As he was about to mount the dun, Dewkes asked, 'What do I do while I'm waiting for you?'

'Get that valise out of sight,' urged Rick. 'No need to hide yourself rightaway. That can wait till we're sure my invitation has been accepted.' He raised his eyes. 'Plenty of foliage on those branches overhanging this clearing. That'd be my choice.'

'All the luck, Sam,' Dewkes said fervently as Rick got mounted.

'Keep your fingers crossed and your eyes peeled,' grinned Rick, and nudged Fernando to movement. 'Be seeing you.'

Well rested and perhaps deriving some small pleasure from this excursion, the dun obliged his rider by proceeding across Bar 9 range at an almost-lively trot. As they drew closer, Rick scanned the set-up. He could see the grazing herd, the main building and the others, the bunkhouse and barn, the usual corrals, and smoke rising from the chimney of the cook-shack. The ranch-house, he noted, was a single-storeyed log and clapboard structure, plank-roofed like the bunkhouse and barn. There was a well-house in the yard between the ranch buildings and the corrals.

They'll have finished breakfast, he guessed. All right, actor. Showtime. Curtain up. And make it a convincing performance.

Rex Abelson and another man emerged from the bunkhouse to follow his approach. He waved to them wearily and stared beyond them. West of the Bar 9 headquarters, his view of the far reaches of the great canyon was blocked by a grassy rise.

The dun toted him into the yard. He reined up a few yards from the foreman and the other man and went into his act.

'Howdy, gents. Niblo's the name. First name Bud. Take it kindly if you'd allow me water my ol' hoss. And there's somethin' you can likely tell me.'

'Think you can make it, Pop?' grinned Abelson. 'To draw water, you got to work the windlass.'

'That takes strength,' drawled the cowhand, as some of his colleagues quit the bunkhouse to appraise the stranger. 'You'll spring a hernia.'

'That's what *you* say, boy,' croaked Rick. 'Well, I ain't ready for the boneyard yet, no siree.'

He made slow work of dismounting and leading the dun to the well, and a convincing show of muscle-strain while turning the handle to hoist up the bucket; he winced and made it appear a mighty effort. While Fernando was slaking his thirst, a heavyset, short-bearded man showed himself on the ranch-house porch. He lit a cigar and studied Rick boredly and Rick made his guess. The boss-man, Luther Prowse.

'Somethin' I can likely tell you, you said,' drawled Abelson. 'What d'you want to know?'

'That big farm back there,' said Rick, jerking a thumb. 'You happen to know him that owns it?'

Prowse answered.

'His name's Kenrick. Why do you want to know?'

'He farms all that land?' prodded Rick. 'Don't do no minin'?'

Abelson was no poker-player. Rick didn't miss the quick glance he aimed at Prowse, whose face was suddenly blank. A sallow-complexioned waddy, tall and thin-lipped, said curtly, 'This canyon's cattle country. No minin' here.'

'Well, by golly, there's gonna be!' cackled Rick, struggling astride Fernando again. 'Mister Kenrick don't know it, but it's there for doggone sure. Gold in them rocks a little way from the crick.'

'You're loco!' growled the sallow man.

'Take it easy, Pete,' ordered Abelson.

'Better forget it, old man,' advised Prowse. 'Either you're near blind or what's left of your sight's playin' tricks on you. And there's laws against bustin' rocks on another man's land. You could be buyin' a lot of trouble for yourself.'

'No, I seen what I seen,' insisted Rick. 'Didn't have to bust no rock, didn't even have to swing my pickaxe. Just leaned against a rock and durned if a piece of it didn't get shoved free. Well, after I spotted good sign, real pay-vein, I stashed that hunk right back where it fell off of. Next, I gotta talk turkey with this Kenrick gent. Fair's fair. The gold's on his land but, if he'll let me dig for it, I'd settle for half – even a quarter.'

'The hell with...!' began the sallow man.

'Will you *shaddup*!' scowled Abelson.

'Only thing....' Rick winced and rubbed at his belly. 'I gotta eat 'fore I parley with the farmer, gotta cook me some grub.' He appealed to the rancher. 'Passed a clump of trees on my way here. Little clearin' inside. That part of your range?' Prowse nodded slowly. 'All right by you if I camp there a spell? Give you my word I won't set fire to the timber. Just gonna make me a cookfire and ...'

'Help yourself,' shrugged Prowse.

'Pow-ful obliged, mister,' grinned Rick, as he began turning the dun. 'Get some beans in me, cuppa java, then look up the farmer and talk a deal. Hot damn! I'm gonna get rich!'

The look the rancher aimed at his men assured him he was in no danger of a bullet in the back. A warning look. He sensed that, as far as Prowse was concerned, 'Bud Niblo' had signed his own death warrant. But no Bar 9 man would be allowed to backshoot him. The sound of the shot could carry a long way and arouse curiosity. He had invited Prowse to dispose of him in his own way and whenever he wished. And given him ample time.

Abelson didn't speak until the eastbound horseman was well out of earshot. Then he swore lucidly. So did Pete Gallard, and the other six hard-cases of Bar 9. Prowse stayed on the porch, puffing on his cigar, staring east through narrowed eyes.

'Of all the crazy, stinkin' luck,' mumbled Abelson. 'For near two years, that chunk's stayed put. Now it's budged again. That old packrat had to lean on it – damn him.'

'It's been our secret ever since,' said Prowse. 'It'll be our secret till after Kenrick quits and it's all my land. He can't hold out much longer. When they hang his kid, Brister'll mount a raid and Kenrick'll be the big loser, his crops, his home, the whole shebang. He'll lose everything.' He chuckled softly. 'And, if he's still alive, I'll play good neighbour and make him a fair offer.'

One of the other men loosed an oath and pointed east.

'Not if Niblo tells him....'

'Niblo won't tell Kenrick anything,' Prowse said steadily. 'Dead men can't talk. Maybe he'll get to eat breakfast, but that'll be his last breakfast. He'll be buried in that clearin'. Rex, you'll have to get rid of the horse too, that crowbait of his.'

'The only way,' Abelson agreed. 'He knows it all, so he's got to go.'

'You got plenty time,' said Prowse. 'Easy chore,

but take Pete with you. You won't need tools. Use the old man's pickaxe and spade. And no hurry. Let him make his fire. He's got time to eat before you shut his mouth.'

'He's mine,' insisted Gallard. 'I owe him – for snoopin' – for findin' what's part mine.'

'Stay patient,' soothed Prowse. 'You'll get your share. Plenty for all of us, the gold we take from them rocks.' To Abelson, he muttered a warning. 'No guns. Some Kenrick hand could hear the shot. Let Pete take care of him. With a knife, he's fast and slick.'

'We'll saddle up, Pete,' said the foreman, and he and Gallard turned and started for the barn.

All the way back to the copse, never once did Rick glance over his shoulder. His confidence was increasing minute by minute. They had bought his spiel, of that he was certain. Were they aware he had so carefully studied reactions? Not likely. Prowse and his men had seen what he meant them to see, an old scarecrow of a fossicker elated at having stumbled on it at last, the end of the rainbow, the pot of gold, every prospector's dream.

When he re-entered the clearing, Dewkes was pacing restlessly. The deputy jerked to a halt, eyeing him expectantly.

'How'd it go?'

'They fell for it, Chris,' Rick declared. 'If I'm wrong about 'em, I won't be followed here.'

'But you believe you're right.'

'I believe I'll have company – the homicidal kind. Got to rustle up a fire now, Chris. It's expected. And, for you, it's that time.'

'Time for me to climb a tree.'

'Choose your hiding place well and be ready to

cover me. I mightn't need your help, but there's just no guessing.'

Dewkes moved through the trees to the south-west edge of the copse to stare across Bar 9 range, while Rick gathered wood, got a small fire going in the centre of the clearing and broke out pan, coffeepot and a can of beans. When he returned, Dewkes retrieved his rifle. The weapon did not encumber him as he climbed a tree to Rick's left, its limbs jutting halfway across the clearing, a green canopy. After he crawled out on to a branch and straddled it, he was invisible; no danger he'd be sighted by riders arriving from whatever direction.

Hunkered, waiting for the beans to heat and the coffee to boil, Rick and the deputy quietly parleyed.

'Oughtn't have to wait long,' Dewkes supposed.

'Not long,' said Rick. 'I told them I'd visit Kenrick as soon as I'm through eating.'

'Not likely the whole bunch'll come for you.'

'I wouldn't think so. Butchering and burying one old fossicker is easy work. One man could handle it. Prowse may send another. I'd say two – three at most.'

'Luther Prowse.' Dewkes was in a mood to spit in disgust, but Rick was almost directly below him. 'More than a few times since he turned Kenrick and Brister against each other, he's claimed he tried to play peacemaker. What a lousy hypocrite.'

'Greed for gold, Chris. It brings out the worst in some.'

'From up here, I can get the drop on 'em.'

'Not rightaway, Chris, not as soon as they show. We need to hear some talk first, let 'em tip their hand. As for answers, you'd better follow my lead.'

'You want *me* to play-act?'

'Nothing to it. The old prospector turns mean, snarls a threat or two. You make a half-hearted attempt to use your authority and restrain me, but then you decide they deserve everything they get – and turn your back. Or you could remove your badge and stow it in your pocket. A gesture'll do it – put the fear of hell into 'em.'

'A bluff play?'

'You catch on fast. Chris, my friend, I believe you're ready.'

'Just as well,' said Dewkes, dropping his voice. 'I hear horses headed this way.'

'Act Three, Scene One,' muttered Rick.

He spooned up beans, munched and swallowed and downed a mouthful of coffee, keeping his ears cocked. The riders were advancing from the ranch headquarters. How many? He listened intently and, as the clip clop of hooves became clearer, decided two. Just fine. Even without the deputy's aid, he could turn the tables on any two killers any time, under any conditions. And these were *his* conditions; he had set up this scene.

Unhurriedly, Abelson and Gallard walked their horses into the clearing and reined up. Rick stayed hunkered, greeting them cheerily.

'Well, howdy again, boys. Light and set. Coffee's hot.'

Gallard leered contemptuously and remarked to Abelson, 'If it was ever gonna happen, wouldn't you guess it'd be a lame-brain like him, an old coot too dumb to think straight?'

'Get it done,' Abelson urged as they dismounted. 'We'll have to dig a hole for him, and I don't wanta be here all mornin'.'

'What – uh – what're you talkin' 'bout?' croaked

Rick, struggling upright, blinking in bewilderment.

'Remember Luther's orders, Pete,' said Abelson. 'Don't use your gun. It's gotta be done quiet.'

'End of the road for you, old-timer,' announced Gallard.

The "old-timer" recoiled in shock as Gallard unsheathed a knife.

'What d'you mean – end of the road?' he whined. 'Hell's sakes, what'd I ever do to you boys?'

'You found somethin' you weren't supposed to,' shrugged Abelson. 'You or anybody else.'

'You mean – the gold?' winced Rick.

'It used to be *our* secret,' grinned Gallard. 'And it's still gonna be.'

Rick pretended to be frozen in shock. He had stepped clear of the fire and stood stooped, gawking at the gleaming blade, letting Gallard advance to within striking distance.

'You can't do it!' he pleaded. 'You can't just – shove your knife in an old man's heart!'

'Won't be aimin' for your heart,' chuckled Gallard. 'I got an easier target – your throat.'

'You can't cut a man's throat from ear to there!' wailed Rick.

Both rogues – Dewkes also – were taken aback by what happened next. As Gallard slashed at him, Rick backstepped nimbly. The blade flashed past his face and then he was swinging his left boot to his would-be murderer's crotch – a savage kick, and well aimed. The effect on Gallard was devastating. He dropped the knife, gasped in anguish, turned from sallow to pasty grey and clutched at his assaulted area. That left him wide open for Rick's bunched right fist, aimed at the point of his chin, an uppercut powered by all his muscle.

Gallard was unconscious before he hit the ground shoulders first. Rallying from his shock, Abelson began drawing his Colt but, at that precise moment, the crackling sound of snapping wood was heard. Deputy Dewkes was realizing, somewhat belatedly, that the limb he had straddled could not support his formidable weight any longer.

Everything came down on Abelson, the branch, the deputy, plus his rifle, before he could leap clear. He was engulfed, pinned down face-first.

Still playing Bud Niblo to the hilt, Rick demanded, 'Who in tarnation're *you* – and how the hell'd you get here?'

Dewkes, struggling to extricate himself from the breakaway branch and all its foliage, retorted, 'How the hell do you *think*? I just dropped in!'

8

No Surrender

There was a livid bump on Abelson's brow. He was dazed for a few moments after Dewkes hauled the branch off him, and those few moments were all the time the deputy needed to transfer the ramrod's Colt from its holster, shove it into his waistband and manacle his prisoner's hands behind his back.

When Abelson's head cleared, his eyes were working again. He gaped at the scarecrow hovering over the unconscious Gallard, brandishing Gallard's own knife.

'He was gonna cut my throat – so I'm gonna cut his!' raged "Old Bud".

'Can't let you do that, old-timer,' Dewkes said sternly. 'I'm an officer of the law and …'

'He ain't woke up,' complained Rick. 'Well, shucks, cuttin' a skunk that ain't gonna feel it's no fun at all.' He turned to glare at the awkwardly squatting Abelson, snarled and bared his teeth, and Abelson was too demoralized to note that, for one so aged, Bud Niblo could boast a full supply of strong white teeth. 'That'un! He was real cool about it, would've stood by while his *compañero* slashed my throat!'

'Now, old-timer ...' began Dewkes.

'Don't you try stoppin' me, Mister Tin Star,' scowled Rick, advancing menacingly. "Less'n this sonofabitch does some explainin', he's dead meat!'

'Damn it, Dewkes, you can't let him...!' began Abelson.

'I just might,' frowned Dewkes. 'Because I'm as curious as he is. He wants answers. I figure he's entitled, Abelson. You'd have watched Gallard butcher him. That bothers me, and there's a lot else bothers me. I was up that tree long enough to hear what you and Gallard said.'

Abelson's scalp crawled as the deputy transferred his star from his vest to a pocket thereof and averted his gaze. Rick lowered himself to one knee, held the point of the blade an inch from his neck and snarled at him, 'There's been feudin' hereabouts. Some ploughboy got back-shot and some young'un called Blister ...'

'Brister,' corrected Dewkes. 'Phil Brister.'

'Wasn't the Brister kid did that shootin' – was it?' demanded Rick, then grimaced impatiently before Abelson could reply. 'Hell, lawboy, he's clammed up. I'm gonna finish him off.'

'Stop him, Dewkes!' cried Abelson.

'Can't hear you,' said Dewkes, shrugging unconcernedly.

'It wasn't Brister.' Abelson's dilated eyes stung from the sweat of his brow trickling into them. 'All right, I've said it. Now take that knife away from the old goat.'

'You ain't sayin' the half of it, you lowdown polecat,' whined Rick. 'You ain't tellin' who *did* kill that sodbuster.'

Abelson nodded toward the still-unconscious Gallard.

'I'll believe that,' said Dewkes. 'But, if you tell me it was Gallard took a shot at Orin Kenrick – that won't be so easy to believe. And, with that knife at your no-good throat, you can't afford to lie.'

'Jorgenson,' winced the ramrod.

'Another Prowse man,' growled Dewkes.

'Aw, hell,' sighed Abelson.

'He don't tell us hardly nothin'!' rasped Rick. So swiftly that Abelson's eyes popped, the knife was transferred to his left hand and his shoulder-holster emptied by his right. That sharp point was again prodding his throat and the .38 was covering the deputy. 'I'm gonna cut him good, lawboy, and don't you get in my way and you ain't wearin' your star anyway!'

'Damn it, old feller, I'm finally getting some answers!' chided Dewkes. 'But I need to know more. If you finish him off now...!' He stared hard at the ramrod. 'Abelson, while there's still time...!'

'All right, all right.' Abelson shrugged helplessly. 'I got – nothin' to win now. We found out about the gold – couple years back – and Luther figured we could have it all, but we needed a plan....'

It spilled out of him in jerky sentences; with that knife at his throat, he was bargaining for his life, his resistance at an end. After the killing of Siddons, Prowse had insisted the harassment should be stepped up. Jorgenson had drawn a killing bead on Orin Kenrick and, when his target pitched from his mount, had made his way home to Bar 9 as Gallard had done. With Phil Brister being held for the Siddons murder, Prowse was eager to throw the Kenricks and Circle B against each other in a bloody fight to the finish.

Bar 9, not Circle B cattle, had been stampeded across Kenrick land, thus triggering the feud. In the time since, Kenrick and Brister men had traded shots from north and south of the creek during the hours of darkness and, in town, had locked horns in violent brawls – pawns in Bar 9's game, all of them. The ultimate object was for Kenrick to be burned out. If that notion didn't occur to Brister during the battle, Prowse men would take care of it. And, if he emerged from all that turmoil alive, Kenrick would be a broken man; it would be the ideal time for Prowse to approach him as a sympathetic neighbour and make an offer.

When Abelson had said it all, the knife was still at his throat. Dewkes said coldly, 'One thing you'd better understand. No use you refusing to repeat your statement to the sheriff and put your name to it. The old man'll be accepted as a reliable witness. You realize that?'

'I know it's all over,' mumbled Abelson. 'I know when I'm licked.'

'That'll do it, I think,' said Rick, reverting to his normal speech; Abelson's jaw sagged.

'That'll do it,' agreed Dewkes.

'Time for you to go fetch your horse,' said Rick. 'You can leave these heroes and their horses to me. Their lariats are all I need. By the time you rejoin me, they'll be well and truly secured.'

'You *ain't old*!' gasped Abelson. 'I've heard that voice before!'

'Be right back,' said Dewkes, and hurried away.

When, a short time later, he led his mount back into the clearing, the prisoners were roped to trees. Gallard had regained consciousness and was in a state of confusion. And as mute as Abelson; Rick had done a thorough job of gagging them. Their horses were tied and Gallard's Colt was thrust in the back of Rick's pants-belt. So he and Dewkes would be packing ample weaponry, he three pistols, Dewkes a pair and his rifle. They mounted. Rick guided Fernando through the trees with the deputy following.

When they had begun their slow crossing of Bar 9 range, Rick paid Dewkes a compliment.

'You did well back there, Chris. Played along with me, picked up all your cues and did some convincing ad-libbing. You could make a career of it. Ever think of becoming an actor?'

'I just want to go on being a deputy sheriff and court and marry Minerva,' muttered Dewkes.

'The way will be clear for you after today,' Rick said encouragingly. 'No feud to cause the lady dismay. Kenrick and Brister – when they're told the truth of the whole affair – will come to terms, and we've cleared Phil Brister already.'

'Sam, it was all for nothing unless we get out of this alive,' warned Dewkes. 'I'm handy with guns, fast when I have to be, but you?'

'I don't think I'll disappoint you,' shrugged Rick. 'Mind a few hints?'

'You've done this before?'

'Let's just say it won't be my debut performance. A tip or two, my friend. We oughtn't to stay mounted when we arrive. A mounted man is too clear a target. You familiar with the Bar 9 layout? There's a well-house that could provide good cover, if you're close enough. Failing that, a corral post'll help.'

'I've been there.'

'If the nearest cover isn't close enough, keep your feet busy. A moving target has a better chance of survival.'

'You're convinced we're headed for a shootout.'

'Chris, when you tell them Abelson confessed everything, do you honestly think they'll submit peacefully?'

'No surrender?'

'Make book on it.'

'You gonna play old Niblo again?'

'Just long enough to cause a little confusion.'

When they were in sight of the ranch buildings, they detected signs of movement. Dewkes caught a flash of sunlight on metal and said grimly, 'They know who's coming. Somebody aimed a spyglass, pair of binoculars, something like that.'

'Uh huh,' grunted Rick. 'We've nailed two. That leaves seven. So, if we can't see all seven of 'em, count on the others covering us from windows or from inside the barn. We play it as they play it.'

Fernando plodded. So did the deputy's horse. They advanced on the five men grouped in the yard, Rick arranging his features in a scowl of indignation, his right hand hanging close to the flap of the rotted canvas concealing the butt of his Colt.

As soon as they were within hearing of Prowse and the other four, he began his harangue, glaring at the rogue-rancher.

'Ain't particular what kinda scum you hire, are you? Couple of 'em rid into my camp and one of 'em tried to damn well butcher me.'

As they reined up, Prowse eyed Dewkes impassively; his enquiry was voiced casually.

'Deputy, what're *you* doin' here?'

'My duty, Luther Prowse,' Dewkes replied, edging his mount close to the well-house. 'Abelson and Gallard weren't counting on my being there. As you can see, they didn't get a chance to silence the old man.'

'I got no notion what Rex and Pete were plannin',' shrugged Prowse.

'You're a stinkin' liar!' raged Rick. 'You sent 'em!'

A lean, hawk-faced hard-case leered derisively and declared, 'This old *hombre*'s tetched in the head, Dewkes. You oughta be smart enough to figure that for yourself.'

'You're Jorgenson,' observed Dewkes. 'The hero who winged Orin Kenrick. It's a little late for you to deny it.' He eyed Prowse coldly. 'A little late for you too. I know it all now, Prowse, how the feud started, who started it – and why.'

'You still ain't makin' sense,' said Prowse. 'We don't know what you're talkin' about.'

'I'm satisfied Abelson knew what *he* was talking about,' retorted Dewkes. 'He made a full confession. Now do I have to explain what that means? It's all over Prowse. You and your whole crew are under arrest.'

'He's bluffin'!' gasped Jorgenson. 'Rex'd never...!'

'But he did,' growled Rick, reverting to his natural voice. 'It took a little persuasion, but Abelson told us everything.'

'Kirby!' Prowse yelled, his hand streaking to his holster.

Rick and the deputy promptly filled their hands and parted company with their horses, Rick going to ground in a bent-legged posture with his Colt at the ready, Dewkes diving for the well-house. For a brief moment, Rick was confused. The first shot had been fired, but by none of the men he could see, and not close at hand. He thought it likely it had been triggered from atop the rise to the west. It sounded like a rifle shot and the shooter was no mean marksman. He caught a blurred impression of a man gripping a six-gun, but not using it, hadn't spotted that one before, because he'd been staked out atop the barn roof. Now he was nosediving from the roof with his left shoulder bloody.

He heeded his own advice and sidestepped hastily, and not a moment too soon. Bar 9 guns were roaring. Prowse's bullet sped past his head as he got off his first shot and made it count. Prowse reeled, his face contorted, his gunhand sagging.

Jorgenson's bullet ricocheted off the windlass and, by then, Dewkes was huddled behind the well-house. From its right side, he aimed fast, squeezed trigger and scored. Jorgenson stumbled backward and flopped, pawing at his chest.

Bullets kicked splinters from a corral post just as Rick reached it. Startling. Intimidating. But, with his life in jeopardy, he couldn't spare time to be either startled or intimidated. His Colt boomed twice and his targets lurched drunkenly and collapsed to the dust.

He heard another pistol roar, heard Dewkes's loud yelp and glimpsed the deputy rolling, his left thigh red-streaked, but his right fist still full of booming .45; the man who had wounded Dewkes died before he sprawled on his back.

'Sam...?' called Dewkes.

'Still here,' Rick replied.

'You been – keeping tally?'

'Making the effort, Chris, but conditions aren't conducive to accurate mathematics.'

The brief silence was broken. Rick heard it again, the distant bark of a rifle, after which the seventh man stumbled from the bunkhouse doorway, wailing, a Winchester slipping from his grasp. From shoulder to wrist, his right arm was red, blood dripping from his agonizing wound. He sagged to his knees, still wailing.

Rick came upright to stare away to the rise. He could see nothing, but his ears caught the receding hoofbeats. The rider was retreating, still invisible, screened by the bulk of the rise.

From the cook-shack, the old chuckboss emerged with his hands up.

'Don't shoot *me*!' he pleaded. 'I dunno nothin' 'bout none of this!'

'I don't have to take you in, old feller,' soothed Dewkes. 'Listen, we'd be obliged for your help. We got dead to be loaded on horses and wounded needing patching before we load *them* on to horses.'

'Do you have a medical kit here?' demanded Rick. 'Deputy Dewkes has a serious leg wound.'

'I'll be fine,' Dewkes said gruffly; he was upright and keeping his weight on his right leg. 'Two holes. Slug must've gone straight through.'

'No chances taken,' insisted Rick. 'Let me at least stem the bleeding.'

The toll was heavy. Prowse and three of his men were dead, the others wounded and incapable of offering further resistance. While the chuckboss did what he could for the other men, Rick concentrated on the entry and exit holes in the deputy's left thigh. It was agreed that, if Dewkes were still conscious after treatment by a Greco doctor, they would offer their report to Whitton in the medico's surgery; Rick could explain everything, but would need Dewkes's support, the sheriff being so wary of him.

Later, after Rick led the laden horses back to the clearing with Dewkes able to sit his own mount again, he rid himself of his aged prospector disguise and changed to Sam Gavin's attire, a transformation witnessed incredulously by Abelson and Gallard. They too were roped to their horses. The journey to Greco was then resumed, interrupted only when they reached that part of the creek's south bank dominated by the cluster of rocks.

Kenrick hands were at work in the fields, but the farmer and his son intercepted the grim procession. The din of gun fire had been heard in the distance and Kenrick demanded an explanation.

'Now it begins,' grouched Dewkes. 'Hell, Sam, we proved we could stop the feud. That's one problem done with, but another starting.'

'Stop the feud?' challenged Kenrick.

'You and Brister were played for suckers – that's the plain truth of it,' Rick told him. To the farmer, he repeated the gist of the statement forced from Abelson, while Jethro stared in wonderment at the rocks. In conclusion, he pointed out, 'The real killer of Joe Siddons, as well as the sniper who wounded Orin, are all through. So Phil Brister has been cleared, and I have two suggestions for you, Mister Kenrick. You have your choices. Either you can ...'

'I'm not gonna turn miner,' growled Kenrick. 'My land's for farmin'.'

'But the word'll spread anyway,' warned Dewkes.

'Impossible to keep it a secret, so why not derive some financial benefit?' urged Rick. 'There'd be mining activity in the high country farther west, I take it?'

'The Corona Hills,' frowned Jethro.

'Surround this rock clump with barbed wire and mount a guard on it,' advised Rick. 'Then visit the Corona Hills diggings and make a deal with some mining company. You don't have to give minehands the run of your entire holding. Offer to lease this specific area, nowhere beyond. State your own terms. Take a lawyer along to keep everything legal. The one named Ingram should be available, because it's for sure his client will be released from the county jail after we return to town.'

'Sounds reasonable to me,' Kenrick said guardedly. 'But you said two suggestions.'

'Disarm yourself,' said Rick. 'Ford the creek, ride to the Brister ranch-house and ...'

'And tell Brister everything Sam's told you,' begged Dewkes. 'Sooner he knows the whole truth, sooner you two'll be peaceful neighbours again.'

'Pa ...' began Jethro.

'I'm doin' it,' decided the farmer. He unstrapped his pistol, detached his sheathed rifle and handed them to his son. 'It wasn't Circle B cattle trampled our crops. I got to acknowledge that to Brister and I don't reckon we'll wrangle – not after I tell him his boy's been cleared.'

'We'd better get going again, Sam,' said Dewkes. 'Got to travel slow, so it'll be afternoon before we see Greco again.'

Around 2.30 that afternoon, in the surgery of another doctor – Dewkes being a tad leery of the irritable Ansell Frickett – his wound was treated and a prognosis offered. Whitton and Schumack were standing by, listening to Rick's account of the gun battle at Bar 9 and the events preceding it. Dewkes had bluntly refused ether, was stubbornly staying conscious and backing Rick's story. Then, before the sheriff could voice his reaction, the doctor had his say.

'No infection. The wound will heal but, though there's no bone damage, vital sinews were torn. Deputy Dewkes will have to rest and, for some time after he's up and about, he'll have to use ...'

'Not a crutch,' pleaded Dewkes.

'A cane then,' said the medico. 'You'll be lame, young man. Maybe not permanently, but we have to be practical. Sheriff Whitton, as a town councilman, I suggest you give some thought to the possibility of a replacement deputy.'

'I don't want to ...' began Dewkes.

'Docs know best, Chris,' said Schumack.

'You're well educated,' the doctor reminded Dewkes. 'There's a suggestion I intend putting to the council, also the school board, an idea about how you'd be better employed. I think it might appeal to you. Meanwhile, I'll help you to my spare bedroom. What you need most right now is rest, and plenty of it.'

'My office,' Whitton growled at Rick. 'Somethin' else you're gonna have to explain to me.'

The county prosecutor, Mat O'Sullivan, was occupying Whitton's desk chair when he re-entered his office with Rick and Schumack in tow. A local JP was perched on the outer edge of the desk, offering an opinion: O'Sullivan was reading an affidavit.

'Signed, sealed and delivered, Mat. It bears Abelson's signature, Gil Keece's and mine. Sure changes everything, doesn't it?'

'You satisfied?' asked Whitton.

'More than,' declared O'Sullivan, surrendering the sheriff's chair. 'Hell of a conspiracy, Ed.'

'The things we never suspect about certain parties,' Whitton said bitterly. 'Luther Prowse for instance.'

'And young Brister wasn't a desperate liar protesting his innocence, told us the truth right from the start,' said O'Sullivan. 'Well, Ed, you have six prisoners, but you ought to have only five. Abelson's confession clears the boy, so ...'

'Bring him out, Gil,' ordered Whitton.

The county attorney and the JP departed. Ushered into the office by the jailer, Phil Brister accepted the return of his personal effects, including his sidearm. As he strapped it on, he assured Whitton, 'Don't worry. No hard feelings on my part. I'm too thankful to be mad at anybody – except the Bar 9 bunch.'

'You know where your horse is stabled, boy,' said Whitton, sinking into his chair. 'Get on home now, tell your father you got fair treatment here – and tell him to cool that hot temper of his.'

Phil donned his hat and remarked, 'I get the feeling I have somebody to thank.'

'Chris Dewkes and him.' Whitton nodded to Rick. 'Name of Gavin, a sportin' man that likes playin' snooper.'

'Mister Gavin ...' began Phil.

'You're welcome,' said Rick. 'And my compliments to your father and brothers. We've met.'

All eyes were on him after Phil walked out. Bluntly, Whitton declared, 'I want to know why, Gavin. You dug deep into the whole lousy mess. You – a gambler. Risked your neck too. Why?

What was in it for you?'

'Just the personal satisfaction,' said Rick. 'I hate feuds as much as you do. I've had experience of other feuds, range wars and such, and seen the misery they can cause, the bloodshed, the tension affecting whole communities. That's what was in it for me. And I call that a fair answer to your question.' He got to his feet. 'If there's nothing else you wish to ask me, I'd like to stop by the Oriental for a much-needed shot of good bourbon.'

'There's nothin' else,' said Whitton. ''Cept thanks.'

'My pleasure,' shrugged Rick.

He toted his valise to the Oriental and was contentedly sipping bourbon when Clint Jarrow joined him to ask, 'What'd she score? Just jack-rabbit? Or did she get lucky and fetch home some quail? She didn't tell me and I forgot to ask. Just returned the rifle I lent her and said see you later.'

'I guess we're talking about Connie,' Rick said mildly. 'I don't know how she made out, Clint, haven't seen her since she got back to town, didn't even know she was out hunting.'

'If she shoots as good as she sings, she's some helluva hunter,' remarked the barkeep.

'That's my friend Connie,' grinned Rick. 'A girl of many talents.'

Entering the hotel soon afterward, he found his wife seated at a table in the lobby, busy with pen, ink and paper.

'Quick letter to you-know-who,' she explained when he paused beside her. 'Just enough to put her mind at ease. The feud over – thanks to your efforts – peace restored and Red Ed in good health, a much relieved lawman.'

'I'll bathe and change,' he said. 'By the time you've mailed that, I'll be back in my room and in the mood for a visitor, but only if you're the visitor.'

'Twenty minutes,' she said, still writing. 'Thirty at most.'

At this time, Mace Kenrick and Buck Brister were still planted in caneback chairs on the porch of the Circle B ranch-house, staring eastward, both recognizing the rider slowly coming into view.

'Your youngest,' observed Kenrick. 'In the clear now, and that's as should be. We got any more beg pardons to trade?'

'I guess not,' sighed Brister. 'We ought to be grateful, when our hired hands traded shots across the creek, their shootin' was wild.'

'It was Prowse's men that shot to kill,' muttered Kenrick. 'Prowse's men that ran cattle through crops of corn and wheat ready for harvestin'. And a Prowse man that gunned poor Joe.'

'What're you gonna do about the gold? Might be a lot of it, or there mightn't be all that much.'

'I'll abide by that gambler's advice.'

'Sly sonofabitch, that Prowse.'

'And greedy.'

'Played one of us against the other. We've been a couple of damn fools.'

'Because,' grouched Kenrick, 'we believed what he wanted us to believe.' He eyed the rancher sidelong. 'Somethin' we'd better be ready for.'

'Meanin' what?' demanded Brister.

'Your youngest and my youngest,' muttered Kenrick. 'They ain't about to change, not the way they feel about each other.'

'That's a fact,' agreed Brister. 'So, if Phil wants to invite your Martha here to socialize with his father and brothers, I won't be objectin'.'

'Best I meet you half-way on that,' decided Kenrick, rising to leave. 'After you're through rejoicin' that his name's been cleared, pass on an invite from me. The Kenricks'd like for him to have supper with us tomorrow night – and you can bet Martha'll cook up somethin' special.'

When ex-Deputy Dewkes awoke from his nap in the doctor's spare bedroom, he found Minerva seated by his cot. She was delighted he had survived the day's violence and was the bearer of interesting news. Mayor Ventry had informed her of the council's intention to add another classroom to the county school. Girls to be separated from the boys. She would continue to teach the girls. Upon his recovery, Chris would be offered the position of teacher and mentor to the male students. The elder boys, it had been decided, needed the guidance of a male teacher who would be as firm with them as was necessary.

'Anything you need to learn about procedure, I can show you,' she smiled.

'That'll be better than carrying a badge,' he said, taking her hand. 'It'll make the courting easier.'

Rick's first question, when his wife joined him, was, 'How was the hunting?'

'My aim was a little off.' She winked and perched on the edge of the bed. 'But I did manage to knock one target off a barn roof and give some pain to another aiming a rifle from a doorway.'

'Couldn't stay out of it, could you?' he challenged.

'You have to admit I was cautious,' she countered. 'Did I get in your way? Did I distract you?'

'Who's complaining?' he grinned. 'You made what could be called a useful contribution right when it mattered most. Nice timing, honey.'

'Do you prefer me as a blonde?' she asked.

'Certainly do,' he nodded. 'The blonde's my wife. Black-haired Connie's just a good friend. I like having a beautiful black-haired friend but – how soon can we head back to Denver without breaking Clint's heart?'

'Let's give it a couple more days,' she suggested. 'Time for Roger Upshaw to publish his big story about the end of the feud. We could mail a copy to the Hargroves, then apologize profusely to Clint, tell him the wanderlust has hit us again and book passage on the next coach for Mendoza Junction.'

'Sounds good to me,' he enthused. 'Any news about Waldo?'

'He'll be my accompanist again tonight,' said Hattie. 'So Sam Gavin will be working a table again.'

'Not the faro layout, I hope,' said Rick. 'Running faro demands intense concentration. I can hear Connie Ross singing, but can't steal time to ogle her.'

'We all have to make sacrifices,' she chuckled.

'Well, that's the detective business for you,' he shrugged.

'That's show business,' she insisted.

'Both, honey,' said Rick. 'Both.'